SIN

LOVE IN MANHATTAN SERIES

DEBORAH BLADON

CHAPTER ONE

LINNY

"IF THIS IS how you dress on Monday morning, I'd love to get a glimpse of you on Saturday night."

I close my eyes even tighter. There's no way he's talking to anyone but me.

His breath inches over the skin of my neck as he whispers, "Just because you can't see me, doesn't mean I can't see you."

I thought he was fast asleep.

When I boarded this flight in New York City two hours ago, the man in the seat next to me was already belted in and silent.

It took me a few minutes to realize that his eyes were shut beneath the dark sunglasses he was wearing.

I used that to my advantage. I spent the first half hour of the flight blatantly staring at him.

Broad shoulders, day-old stubble covering his jaw, brown hair that is messed up just enough to promise a sexy, bad-boy beneath the tailored gray suit, black dress shirt and expensive tie.

"I'm West." His deep baritone voice rumbles through every part of me.

If I could orgasm just from a man's voice, this would be the one.

"And you are?" he continues talking even though I'm clearly not responding to him. "You're not asleep. You can stop pretending you are."

I bite the bullet and open my eyes. I turn to look at him.

Holy hell.

I thought this man was hot when he was wearing sunglasses.

His warm brown eyes add another dimension to how devastatingly gorgeous he is.

"What's your name?" He looks into my green eyes before his gaze travels over my shoulder length brown hair.

I turn my head so I'm facing forward again. I was the odd woman out when my friends and I decided to take this trip to Las Vegas. After a quick game of rock-paper-scissors, they lucked out and are sitting next to each other in the third row.

I was stuck with this aisle seat in the first row next to this stranger.

I can't decide if that's a bad thing or a very good thing.

"We'll revisit the name issue." He slides his hand to the armrest until it's just mere inches from mine. "I need a vodka."

"It's ten in the morning," I point out.

I catch a side glimpse of him sliding up the sleeve of his suit jacket to look at a silver watch. "In New York. It's three in the afternoon in London so cheers."

The flight attendant is pushing a glass of clear liquid into his hand before I can absorb what he just said.

First class definitely comes with perks.

"Can I get you anything?" She looks me over trying to hide the smirk that's tugging at her lips.

One dose of self-esteem with a chaser of courage, please.

I wish that were on the drink menu.

"She'll take one of these," West says.

"I don't day drink." I glance in his direction again.

"You're fucking kidding me." He lets out a husky laugh. "You were sober when you got dressed this morning?"

I look down at the tight white tank top, bright pink tutu and white high heels I'm wearing.

Thank God I tucked the tiara that was on my head back into my bag after my friends took their seats.

"I'm not the only one dressed like this." I jerk a thumb over my shoulder. "There are two other women on this flight dressed just like me."

The plan we hatched a week ago seemed sane at the time.

Our mutual friend, Kendra, is set to marry her fiancé in less than a month. Since we're all bridesmaids, we thought it would be fun to plan a one-night-only bachelorette party.

Unfortunately, the only night our schedules synced up was tonight.

We told the bride-to-be to meet us at the airport in Vegas since her flight from Atlanta lands thirty minutes before our flight. She has no idea that we'll all be dressed in the same over-the-top outfit she wore in the pictures she posted to social media to announce her engagement.

That part of the plan was not my idea. I was outvoted. Twice.

"I don't care about them." He leans so close to me that his lips almost touch mine. "Something tells me that you're the one who is unforgettable."

How in the hell is this happening? This handsome

stranger is flirting with me while I'm dressed like I'm about to hit up a Halloween party.

"Do you want a vodka or not, Miss?" The flight attendant interrupts the moment with her snippy tone and unwelcome question.

West doesn't break our gaze as he polishes off his drink in one swallow. "Bring this angel a glass of vodka and a glass of orange juice. She'd like both."

I'd like neither, but I'm too stunned to form any words. *Angel*? Did he just call me an angel?

My gaze drifts to the flight attendant as she takes his empty glass and then steps toward the galley. When she disappears from view I turn and lock eyes with West again. "I was serious when I said I don't drink during the day."

"You're headed to Sin City." He glances briefly out the window next to him at the blue sky and wispy clouds. "You're missing out on half the fun if you don't drink before the sun sets."

I attempt to smooth down the tulle of my skirt, but it's useless. It's just my luck to meet the hottest man I've ever laid eyes on when I'm wearing this getup. Why can't I cross paths with a man like this when I'm tucked into one of the tailored suits or dresses that are waiting for me back in my closet in Manhattan?

I feel a sudden need to explain my current wardrobe choice to him. "I don't usually dress like this. I'm meeting someone at the airport and this is part of the surprise."

He studies me, his gaze focused on my face. "The other two women you mentioned are in on this?"

I nod, feeling a spark of relief that he's seeing a glimpse of who I really am. I shouldn't care what he thinks of me, but I don't want him walking off this airplane with the impression that I'm a woman who parties non-stop in Vegas.

"That's one lucky bastard you're meeting," he says smoothly with a lift of his brow.

The flight attendant appears again with two glasses in her hands. She places them both down on the wide armrest between West and me.

"Do you and your angel need anything else, West?" Sarcasm laces every single one of her words.

"Not at the moment, Sara, but I'll let you know if that changes."

I glance at the two glasses as she walks away before I turn my attention back to him. "I'm not drinking either of those and for the record, I'm going to Vegas to celebrate with my friends. There's no lucky bastard waiting for me there."

His lips curve up in an almost smile. "You're wrong about that. There will be a lucky bastard waiting for you tonight at the Echo Resort and Casino. It's on the strip."

My gaze darts over his face. "What are you talking about?"

"I'm staying there." He downs the vodka in my glass in one swallow. "I'll be in room 2626. When you're done with your day of celebration, join me for a night of sin."

I laugh. "I'm not that type of woman…I mean, I don't and I can't."

What I really mean is that I've never spent a night with a man I don't know, but I'm not about to confess that to a complete stranger.

He looks down at where my hands are laced together in my lap. "I don't see a ring. Are you married? Engaged? In a relationship?"

"No, no and no," I spit back before I pick up the glass of orange juice and drink it all. I wish to hell I had gotten my hands on the vodka before he did. "Are you in a relationship?"

"If I were in a relationship, I wouldn't have invited you to my room." He tucks a lock of my hair behind my ear. "You know what they say about Vegas."

"That what happens there stays there?" I don't move back from his touch even though my common sense is screaming at me to turn around and stop talking to him.

"You can live out every fantasy you have there, and no one will be the wiser." The pad of his thumb brushes my bottom lip. "You'll go on with your life tomorrow. I'll go on with mine and you'll have a Vegas memory you'll never forget."

They aren't just sweet words meant to tempt me. There's a promise there too. I see it in the way he's looking at me.

"Miss?" Sara, the flight attendant, is standing at my side, her fingers strumming over my shoulder. "Your friends have persuaded the man sitting across the aisle from them to switch seats with you. Normally, I wouldn't be so accommodating, but I'm willing to make an exception this one time."

Dammit.

I unbuckle my seatbelt. Two hours ago I wanted desperately to sit closer to my friends. Now, I'd be happy staying in place until the plane lands.

"It was a pleasure." West lifts my hand to his lips and kisses it softly. "I'll see you tonight, angel."

I stand, smiling softly. It's not a question. It's an assumption. As tempting as his invitation is, I doubt I'll ever see this man again. He doesn't realize it, but he's already given me a memory that I'll cherish for a lifetime.

CHAPTER TWO

LINNY

"CAN we change before we go to dinner?" I glance down at the wrinkled tank top and the tulle skirt that now has a tattered hem. I don't have to look in a mirror to know that I resemble a wreck. The plastic tiara on my head isn't doing my appearance any favors.

The only consolation is that we're in a casino and since this is Vegas, we haven't gotten more than a half dozen second glances. Most people have passed us by without even looking in our direction.

Kendra Baldwin, the soon-to-be-bride, shakes her head vehemently as she scans a row of blackjack tables. "You can't possibly know how much it means to me that my three best friends went to all this trouble. Besides, I'm the one who looks the most ridiculous out of all of us."

I quickly glance at my fellow bridesmaids, Harmony Curry and Priscilla Mata. They're dressed in outfits that match my own. The only difference between the three of us is

Harmony's shirt. She's bunched the front of it into a knot just below her breasts so she can show off her toned stomach.

Kendra looks like a dream in a short white lace dress. There's a pink sash draped over her shoulder with the words *The Bride* written in red lettering. That's courtesy of Priscilla. She had it tucked in her suitcase.

The tiara propped atop Kendra's long red locks is semi-real. It was a gift from a long lost relative of hers that descended from royalty. It's crafted from silver and a handful of small diamonds that are lost among the dozens of round cubic zirconia stones that sparkle in any available light.

Harmony insisted that Kendra bring the tiara to Las Vegas. She told her that she wanted to get a closer look at it after seeing it in the engagement picture. It was all part of our plan to surprise her. Harmony demanded that Kendra wear it as soon as we got to our hotel earlier. It hasn't left her head since.

"You look like triplets." Kendra takes a sip of the margarita in her hand. Priscilla ordered it an hour ago. It's in a plastic souvenir cup that's shaped like the Eiffel Tower in honor of Kendra's honeymoon destination. She'll be jetting off to Paris the day after the wedding for a weeklong adventure in the City of Lights.

Harmony steals a quick glance at Priscilla and me. "We're all brunettes. We're all wearing the same outfit. That's where the similarities end."

She's right.

"I choked up the minute I saw the three of you in the airport this morning." Kendra's voice quivers. "Maybe you don't look like triplets, but you do look like the three best friends a girl could ever ask for."

Those words held more weight eight years ago than they do today. That was before we graduated from our Manhattan high school. Back then on the last day of classes, Kendra made the three of us a promise that we'd be bridesmaids in her wedding.

I was sure she'd forgotten about it until she called me the day after her engagement to remind me that I would be in her bridal party, standing alongside Harmony and Priscilla. Kendra's sister, Daphne, is the matron-of-honor. The only reason she's not living it up in Vegas with us tonight is she gave birth to her first baby a week ago.

The sound of a slot machine ringing an alarm blares in the distance. We all steal a quick glance in that direction. It's a sign of someone's luck. Unfortunately, the four of us didn't fare as well. We each brought extra money to Vegas to play the slots, but one-by-one we left our machines empty-handed. I only lost twenty dollars. Kendra's toll so far is seventy-five dollars gone.

"You didn't even notice us when we got off the plane, Kendra." Priscilla sighs. "You had your back turned to us and didn't hear me when I called your name. What the hell were you staring at?"

Kendra's cheeks turn pink as her gaze drops to the carpeted floor. "I shouldn't say."

That's Kendra code for *push me to confess*.

She used the same line on us back in twelfth grade when we cornered her at lunch to ask if she'd hooked up with Danny Keller after prom. She had. She's marrying him less than a month from now.

'*I shouldn't say*' has been her go-to every time she's wanted to tell us something but needs some subtle persuasion to get the words out.

"What were you looking at, Kendra?" I ask in a gentle tone. "You know you can tell us. We're bound to secrecy."

We're not bound to anything but the ties of our friendship.

They're still solid, although time and distance have weakened them. This is the first time the four of us have been together since Priscilla's wedding two years ago. Before that, we reunited the day Harmony said I do.

Although Harmony lives in New Jersey and Priscilla calls upstate New York her home now, we rarely get together. Their lives consist of husbands, kids and their careers. Their free time is precious and even though they're on summer break right now, it still took some coaxing to get them to agree to drop everything to jet off to Vegas for twenty-four hours.

"Do you all know what a hall pass is?" Kendra asks, her tone soft.

Priscilla rolls her eyes. "I thought we agreed not to talk shop in front of Linny. She doesn't understand teacher lingo the way the three of us do."

I shake my head causing the tiara to shift slightly. It felt like Kendra jammed the plastic combs on the sides of it into my scalp when she put it back on my head after I took it off two hours ago.

"It's not teacher lingo," I scoff, irritated that Priscilla has once again found a way to remind me that I didn't follow the same career path as the three of them. They all teach in grade schools. I work in advertising. "Kendra is talking about a sexual hall pass."

"A what?" Priscilla's brow furrows. "What the hell is a sexual hall pass?"

"Someone you're allowed to fuck if you get the chance," Harmony pipes up. "Mine is Trey Hale, the baseball player. Rueben's is Libby Duncan, the Broadway actress."

"Your husband's dream fuck is Libby Duncan?" I grin. "Is that why you asked me if I could get tickets to that musical she was headlining?"

"He's her biggest fan. She's as happily married as Rueben and I are, so she's never going to be his hall pass. I knew he'd get a thrill out of being in the same theatre as her." Harmony's eyes light up as she talks about her husband.

I sigh and wrap my arm around her shoulder.

When Harmony texted me six months ago to ask if I could use my connections to find two tickets to Libby's sold out show, I did. I also offered my place to her for the night she was crossing the bridge into Manhattan with Reuben.

I was in New Orleans for business and I knew that she'd appreciate the chance to leave her two-year-old son with his grandma while she spent an entire night uninterrupted with her husband. When I returned from my trip she told me it was the best night she'd had in years.

"My new hall pass is the first person who walked off your flight." Kendra fans her hand in front of her face as if she's cooling herself down. "That was a mighty fine man. Dark hair, sunglasses, gray suit, and a killer smile."

Priscilla steps forward. "You have to be talking about the guy Linny was sitting next to at the start of our flight. He was already in his seat with those sunglasses on."

"He was asleep." Harmony shrugs. "He never had the pleasure of meeting our beautiful Lincoln Dawn Faye."

"I did meet him."

All three of my friends turn to look at me.

Kendra is the first one to say anything. "You met him? What's his name? Is he married or single? Did you get his number?"

I raise both hands in the air hoping to ward off more questions. "Slow down."

"He woke up?" Priscilla points at me. "Why the hell didn't we hear about this sooner? We've been together all day and you didn't think to mention it?"

I point a finger back at her. "We're here to celebrate Kendra's engagement, not to talk about a random guy I sat next to on an airplane."

"What's his name, Linny?"

I glance over at Kendra to see an expectant look on her face. It's the second time she's asked me the question, so I answer. "West."

"West?" she repeats back. "West what?"

I shrug. "Just West."

"Mysterious," Harmony says as she takes Kendra's drink from her and downs a gulp. "Is he from New York?"

"I have no idea." My lips twitch. "We only exchanged a few words and then I moved to the seat across the aisle from the two of you."

"Is his voice as sexy as I imagine it is?" Kendra looks me in the eye. "It's deep, isn't it?"

I scratch my eyebrow. I'm not going to confess that his voice was the most seductive I've ever heard. That will only open another floodgate and a barrage of new questions will be fired my way at ward speed. "He has a nice voice."

"Did he at least ask for your number?" Harmony fingers the tulle on the front of her skirt as her blue eyes rake me over. "You look like every guy's dream today, Linny. Tell me he wanted to see you again."

I blush at the compliment.

"Hold that thought." Kendra nudges her shoulder into mine. "We have a dinner reservation in ten minutes. We need to pile into a cab and head up the strip."

"Let's go back to the hotel and change first." I clasp my hands together in front of me. "Please, Kendra."

"That's not happening." Harmony slips her hand into mine. "We're wearing our tutus and tiaras to dinner and we're keeping them on for the surprise I arranged for all of us."

"What surprise?" I toss her a skeptical look as a knot forms in the pit of my stomach. I hate surprises. She knows that.

"You'll have to wait and see." She tugs on my hand. "I guarantee we're all going to love it."

CHAPTER THREE

JEREMY

"JEREMY WESTON." I extend my hand to the gray-haired man in the navy blue plaid suit who just introduced himself to me. "It's good to meet you, Jim."

He's the owner of this restaurant, and we share a common interest. Our mutual business partner, Rocco Jones, has already arrived for dinner. He's sitting at a table next to a bank of windows that overlooks the Las Vegas strip.

I don't have a share in this restaurant and Jim doesn't own a red cent of my company, Rizon Vodka, but Rocco had a hand in the success of both.

"What's he drinking?" I point at Rocco.

Jim laughs. "Rizon Vodka."

I rest a hand on his shoulder and squeeze it. "Looks like he's doing us both a favor tonight."

Jim nudges his dark-framed eyeglasses up his nose with a push of his finger. "The meal and the drinks are on the house. Rocco insisted. I'll take it out of his cut."

I smile inwardly. "I'll see myself to the table."

As I near the table I'm greeted with the sound of female laughter. I look to my left to find three women seated at the bar. Their backs are to the bartender. Their eyes are pinned on Rocco.

He's wearing a pair of jeans and a black T-shirt. He looks out of place in this five-star eatery, yet he seems more at ease than anyone else.

I tug my tie from my neck and tuck it into my jacket pocket.

"Don't hide that tie. I have a better place for it."

I turn at the sound of the breathy voice that just tossed those words in my direction.

A pretty blonde has her hands clasped together in front of her. "It would look perfect wrapped around my wrists."

Her friends let out a chorus of giggles and one hoots for good measure.

I give them one of my dimpled smiles and carry on.

Rocco's on his feet by the time I reach his table. "Sounds like you're making plans for later."

I shake his hand and pat him on the back when he goes in for a hug. "You know Vegas. Everyone is up for anything."

He eyes the women at the bar. "They are. They invited me to join them when I arrived."

"Yet you're sitting all by your lonesome, old man," I joke. "You don't think you have the stamina for all three of them?"

Rocco's thirty-four and he's accomplished more in his life than most people twice his age. He was a professional poker champion before he dove into the world of investing in other people's dreams.

He's brought mine to fruition and I couldn't be more grateful. He knows it. I know he doesn't mind when I goad him about his age.

"If I invited them back to my hotel room, I guarantee no one would leave with a complaint," he says, motioning for me to take the seat across the table from him.

He waits for me to sit before he does the same.

"I doubt like hell you could make that claim, Jeremy." He takes a sip of our prize-winning vodka. "You're what now? Twenty-two?"

I shake my head, laughing. "You know I'm twenty-nine, you bastard."

His hand is in the air motioning to someone to bring a drink for me. "I take it you're drinking Rizon tonight?"

"Every chance I get." I lean back in the chair. "How is it that you can conduct business all day dressed like that and I had to wear a fucking suit?"

The two suits I packed weren't designed for Nevada heat in mid-June.

"That privilege comes with age, young man." His blue eyes rake me over. "Give yourself a few years and a few million more in your bank account and you too can leave your suits back in Manhattan when you head west."

"You've given me yet another reason to work my ass off." I grin as the server places a glass of vodka in front of me on the table. "Thank you."

She rests her hand on my shoulder, smiling in appreciation. "The chef is preparing the daily special for you both as requested by Mr. Jones. I hope you like grilled octopus, sir."

I look over at Rocco before I glance back at the server. She's barely legal age. I swear I can see imprints on her perfect white teeth from where braces once sat. She'll get chewed up and spit out in this town in no time flat.

I inch back far enough that her hand falls. "That's fine."

Her hazel eyes lock on mine. "Do you need anything else from me?"

"We're good, Sherri," Rocco interjects. "You're needed at table twelve."

Her gaze darts to Rocco. "Of course, sir. I'll take care of that now."

Rocco watches as she walks away. "I'm working with the management team to lower the turnover rate. It's why I flew here two days ago."

"You can't hold onto employees?" I sip the vodka, the familiar taste rousing my taste buds.

"I've had the same assistant for seven years." He rakes a hand through his dark brown hair. "I pay him well and give him ample time off. This place pays shit and overworks everyone they hire. That stops today."

"You're in town to drop the hammer?" I look over at the bar and the women who are still blatantly gawking at us. "You're going to mix some pleasure with that business, aren't you?"

His gaze follows mine. "If I do it won't be with any of them. What about you?"

The only pleasure I'm interested in involves the gorgeous brunette I met on the airplane this morning.

Time will tell if she takes me up on my invitation to join me in my room tonight.

"I may have plans later."

"May have?" He asks as he watches Sherri greet the couple that just took their seats at a table near us. "You didn't lock it down?"

I ignore the question to focus on the reason for this dinner.

I asked for a face-to-face with Rocco back in New York City last week to go over the details of a new product we're launching in the fall. He was already committed to non-stop meetings, so we scheduled for next week.

When I mentioned in a text message that I was heading to Vegas to meet with a casino owner about serving Rizon products exclusively in his properties, Rocco told me he was on his way here too.

He suggested we talk over dinner, so here we are.

"What did you think of that sample bottle I sent you two weeks ago?" I look out at the bright lights lining the strip.

"It was excellent. I think you found our winner."

I trust his judgment, but I trust my instinct even more. Since I took over running the company from the interim CEO my grandfather appointed before his death, I've branched out from our traditional vodka to a host of flavors.

The timing was ideal and our market share has steadily increased since. Our smooth vanilla vodka is set to be the newest notch in our belt.

"I'm glad we're on the same page." I raise my glass in the air. "Here's to another successful launch."

He taps his glass against mine before he tosses back the rest of his drink. "We need the launch of this to be in a different league. Throw me every idea you've got."

I lean back in my chair and smile. "Buckle up. We're about to bury every other vanilla vodka out there."

CHAPTER FOUR

LINNY

HARMONY WAS ONLY PARTIALLY RIGHT. She's enjoying the surprise she arranged. Priscilla is too. Kendra is having the time of her life, but I wish I were anywhere but here.

An incredibly muscular almost-naked man spins in front of me before his left hand dives into the front of the tight, white briefs he's wearing. He cups the obvious bulge.

His blue eyes sparkle as he shoots me a wink while he skims his tongue over his bottom lip.

"Do you want a lap dance, love?" His voice is calm and controlled. It carries over the loud music that Harmony is streaming from her phone into a mini speaker on top of the bar.

We're in the main room of the luxury three-bedroom suite we rented for the night.

My friends are dancing in a circle. In the middle is a tall

blond-haired man with abs for days and an ass that Priscilla can't keep her eyes off of.

The blond introduced himself as Jay. The man with the black hair who is fondling himself in front of me is Ray.

Jay and Ray. Two strippers for one low price.

That's what Harmony whispered in my ear when Kendra opened the door to the suite with a squeal when she saw the men standing there dressed as police officers with wicked grins on their faces.

I flick my hand in the air toward Ray. "You can go join the party over there. I'm fine here."

He shakes his head. "You've been my favorite since I got here. You're the most beautiful woman I've seen."

Tonight? In the last hour? The last twenty seconds?

I know he's paid to make every woman feel special and I have to admit, he's good-looking and built in every way that matters.

My eyes linger on the front of his briefs as he slides his hand out.

He's hard and large. His erection is straining against the thin white fabric.

I take one last glance at the dark hair that trails beneath his briefs.

"Come dance with me." He holds out his hand. "I'm paid not to behave, but for you, I'll be a gentleman."

I spot Kendra waving me over with both of her hands. This is her special night. In just a few weeks, she's going to marry the love of her life and start a new chapter. I don't want to blemish her memory of this trip by being the one bridesmaid who wouldn't let loose and have fun.

I reach for Ray's hand and tug him over to where everyone is dancing. I take a spot next to Kendra, tossing my arms in the air. I sway to the music and finally let myself get lost in the moment.

———

"HOW OLD ARE YOU, LINCOLN?"

Ray joins me near the large window of the suite. It offers a breathtaking view of the lights of the strip. This city never quiets. The raw energy here is palpable regardless of what time of day it is.

It's past midnight and our dance party is finally winding down.

There was plenty of champagne and loads of innuendo.

Ray made it clear an hour ago that he'd love to join me in one of the bedrooms for a private dance. My three friends thought it was the best idea they'd heard all day.

I've never slept with a stripper. That might be because I've never met one until tonight.

"It's rude to ask that, isn't it?" I laugh as I take a sip of water from a bottle I found in the mini fridge. I doubt it's complimentary, but this trip to Vegas is as much a treat for myself as it is a celebration for Kendra.

I needed a break from my life in Manhattan and what better place to do that than Sin City?

He zips up the fly on his pants and starts buttoning his shirt. "Some women prefer if a guy asks. They think it's rude to assume."

"I'm twenty-six." I tilt my head and study his face. "How old are you?"

He smirks. "Take a guess."

I pivot so I'm facing him directly. I look over his features. His brow and jawline are strong. His lips are thin. They're nothing like West's lips.

I close my eyes in a useless attempt to brush away the memory of the man I met on the airplane. His handsome face and the sound of his voice have invaded my thoughts all day.

On the way back to the hotel after dinner, I stared out the window of the taxi as we passed the Echo Resort and Casino. I looked up as I tried in vain to pinpoint the twenty-sixth floor before the light changed from red to green and our car sped away.

"I'll give you a hint." Ray tucks the tail of his shirt into his pants. "I'm older than twenty-eight but younger than thirty."

I glance over his shoulder to see my three friends staring at us.

They had their innocent fun earlier when they danced with Jay. He gave each of them some one-on-one attention, but he kept his black briefs on the entire time.

He offered to drop them more than once, but Kendra waved that idea away with a quick swat of her hand on his chest telling him that the only dick she's ever seen is Danny Keller's and she doesn't want that to change.

The wild stripper party Harmony bought and paid for has ended up being as tame as the dances we all went to in high school.

"I get that you're not interested in a hook-up." He smiles softly. "Let's go grab a drink. We'll leave your three friends here if that's all right by you."

I laugh. A drink wouldn't hurt and it would give me a chance to unwind without the cheerful chatter about next year's lesson plans that I've been subjected to all day. My friends may have the summer off, but they love their jobs enough to bring their excitement about next term along on our mini-vacation.

"Just a drink?" I look down at the tank top and tutu I'm still wearing. "I should change first."

"There's a costume party happening down the strip right now." He rubs his jaw. "It's at a club inside the Echo Resort. I can get us in and if we stay dressed like we are, we'll each score a free drink."

Echo Resort and Casino. That's where West is staying.

"I'm not trying to keep you in that hot little skirt because it drives me crazy." He wiggles both brows. "I swear there's a costume party tonight. It's a promo thing for a new tequila."

"Go!" Kendra yells from where she's standing with Harmony and Priscilla. "We're all calling it a night. Go and have fun, Linny."

I glance at their smiling faces before I turn back to Ray. "Looks like we're headed to the Echo Resort."

CHAPTER FIVE

LINNY

I STAND in front of the door to Room 2626 at the Echo Resort and chew on the corner of my bottom lip. I shouldn't even be here.

It's past two a.m. and I'm in a restricted area.

You need a room key card to access the elevator that leads up here.

I obviously don't have one of those since I'm staying at the Vertex Hotel.

The man I came to this resort with did have one.

Ray tugged a key card for the hotel from his wallet when I told him about West. He handed me the card after explaining that he'd gotten it two weeks ago from a woman on the thirty-second floor who invited him back to her room after a lap dance at the club he works at three nights a week.

He used the card that night. After he gave her an hour-and-a-half of his time and some extra special treatment, he tucked the card back into his wallet and left with a hefty tip.

He told me he meant to toss it in the trash but never got around to it. It's expired, but it does bear the name and logo of this resort.

I was shaking as I neared the elevator after saying goodbye to Ray. He left me with a kiss on the back of my hand and assurance that I was doing the right thing by heading up to West's room.

I barely know Ray and we only shared one drink, but I took his advice. He told me that there's no harm in having fun with a stranger.

He's right.

I want to see West again and so I took the card, marched up to the guard standing by the elevator and as one of the three women in front of me flashed him a look at her key card, I asked another of the women where she bought her red dress.

I didn't have to show the card I was clutching tightly in my hand.

Instead, I boarded the lift and listened to a stranger talk about her favorite clothing boutique in Los Angeles.

She spun in a circle as the elevator's doors closed, showing off the dress that she had paired with a red facemask trimmed with feathers to create a costume for the party. She looked elegant and sexy.

She giggled at my tutu and tiara as her friend used her key card to scan the pad in the elevator. She pressed the button for the twenty-ninth floor and I pushed the button that read twenty-six.

Once the doors popped open, the trio blew me a flurry of air kisses as I stepped out into the quiet corridor.

I've been standing here for what feels like an hour, but it can't be more than a few minutes.

I take a deep breath and knock softly on the door to West's room.

I wait at least ten seconds.

Nothing happens.

I knock again, a touch louder this time. I take a step back so if he gazes out the door's peephole he'll see my tank top and tutu.

At least a minute passes without any response.

I inch forward again, but this time I rest my ear against the heavy steel door.

Not surprisingly, I hear absolutely nothing.

Maybe he's asleep. Or maybe this isn't his room at all.

Dammit.

What if he gave me a random hotel name and room number because he's an asshole who likes to toy with women?

I shake my head. I knew this was a bad idea. I've never had good luck in Las Vegas with men. Why would that change now?

I curse myself for being so naïve and just as I'm about to step away from the door, I hear the unmistakable sound of the lock turning.

Whoever is in this room is about to give me hell for waking them up and I deserve it.

I brace myself for their wrath just as the door flies open.

It's him.

West is standing in front of me with his hair a mess, his eyes heavy from sleep and his leanly muscular body exposed except for what's hidden under his black boxer briefs.

He rubs his hand over his eyes. "Tell me I'm not dreaming."

I scan every inch of him again. *Wow. This man is beautiful.*

"You're hotter than the strippers I saw earlier." The words tumble out of my mouth before I can stop them.

His lips curve into a wicked grin. "Hello to you too, angel. Come on in."

———

"THE TIARA IS A NICE TOUCH." He crosses his arms over his chest as he nudges his chin up. "Did you add that just for me?"

I reach up and tug it off my head before I toss it on a sleek wooden table just inside the entrance to his suite.

The light is dim, but I can make out how delicious his thick biceps look, and his sculpted abs. His legs are toned and his chest is broad and smooth.

"Do you like what you see?"

I blush when I realize I've been blatantly staring at the man again.

"I'm sorry I woke you." I hold my small white clutch purse against my stomach. I don't have any abs, although I don't think he'll care about that. "I shouldn't have come so late."

"I'm glad you woke me up." He uncrosses his arms and gestures toward the expansive living room of the suite. "Can I get you something to drink?"

I skim my tongue over my bottom lip. "Some water if it's not too much trouble."

He stalks across the room to a bar area. He opens a mini fridge and grabs a small bottle of water. By the time he's back in front of me, he's cracked the seal on the lid.

"Here you go, angel."

"Angel," I repeat back as I take the bottle from him. I'm

dying to ask him if it's a nickname he calls every woman he meets, but I stop myself.

"You looked like an angel when I opened my eyes this morning." He stares down at me. "The last thing I excepted to see when I woke up on that flight was a woman as beautiful as you."

Charm. It's oozing off of him, along with an undeniable primal masculine energy.

"I like it," I confess.

He watches me closely as I take a long sip of the water. "I crashed about an hour ago because I didn't think you'd show up."

I don't protest as he tugs the bottle from my hand and finishes what's left. "I was busy earlier."

"Watching strippers." His gravelly voice sends a shiver down my spine.

My nipples are hard and straining against the thin cotton tank top and the white lace of my bra. I'm wound up tight and the man hasn't even touched me yet. "I'm in Vegas for a bachelorette party."

"On the flight this morning you said you weren't engaged, so am I safe to assume you're not the blushing bride-to-be?" He widens his stance.

I keep my eyes locked on his as I answer. "I'm a bridesmaid."

He steps closer. "I told you I was a lucky bastard. I hit the jackpot tonight."

CHAPTER SIX

JEREMY

I WOULD HAVE a bet a thousand dollars that she wasn't going to show, yet here she is.

I'm right in front of her. She looks different than she did this morning when her smoky eye shadow was perfectly applied and a light layer of pink gloss covered her lips.

I like this version of her even more with her makeup smudged. Earlier I didn't notice the light dusting of freckles that covers her nose and trails over her cheeks.

She's a beauty by any measure.

"What's your name?" I ask as I lift a finger to her chin.

She flinches only slightly. "Angel."

"So you're going to stick with that?" I slide my fingers to her neck and beyond to her silky brown hair. I fist it in my hand, angling her head back.

A little moan escapes her lips. "Are you going to kiss me?"

I lean forward so I can rub the tip of my nose along the soft skin of her neck. "I'll start with that."

I do. I trail kisses over her neck, taking my time until I reach her chin. Before I claim her mouth, I look into her light green eyes. "You're shaking. Are you sure you want to do this?"

"I'm excited," she blurts out with a small whimper. "I want this. I'm sure. I'm very sure."

That's all the reassurance I need.

I take her face in my hands, tilting her head slightly before I seal my mouth over hers.

———

MY SKIN HEATS as she parts her soft lips to let me inside. I dive in, my tongue against hers, my teeth seeking out her flesh.

She beats me to it and tugs my bottom lip between her teeth.

My dick is instantly hard; harder than it was when I saw her standing on the other side of the hotel room door.

I slide one hand down her body, stopping to squeeze her waist before I grab the back of her thigh.

Skin as soft and smooth as silk awaits me.

My cock throbs as I urge her against me.

She purrs like a kitten when I tighten my fingers over the curve of her ass.

I feel lace panties. I want those on the floor.

"I can't believe I'm doing this," she whispers as her hands roam my shoulders before they slide down my arms.

I want to be a memory this woman will never forget so I kiss her again, deeper this time. My tongue seeks out more. I taste tequila mixed with mint and a sweet note that has to be just her.

I break the kiss and trail my lips over her cheek until they're resting against her ear. "I'm aching for you."

"I'm ready if you are," she says in a breathy tone.

I hold back a chuckle. She's a bundle of nerves. "We're just getting started, angel. There are so many things I want to do with you."

"Like what?" she asks in a whimper.

"We'll start with this." I move my hand to her waist and tug on the bottom of her tank top. I've been dying to see her tits all day. I can tell they're more than a handful. "Take off your shirt."

Her eyes widen as she takes a small step back. "I'm not perfect."

Jesus. Where the fuck did that come from?

I cup her face in my hands and kiss her again. This time it's slow and sensual. "You're beautiful."

Her lips curve up into a soft smile. "So are you."

I watch as she grabs the hem of the shirt with both hands before she slides it up and over her head. The motion messes her hair. She's already got a sexy just-fucked look and I've barely touched her.

"The bra too." I fist my hands at my sides. I want to touch her, but I know if I do, I'll lose it. I'll carry her to the bed, slide on a condom and fuck her senseless.

I want that, but I want this more.

I have all night. She's mine until the morning.

She slides her bra off in a rush, her hands darting to cover two plump breasts with high peaked nipples.

I reach forward and take her wrists in my hands. Resistance is there, but I tug them away from her skin. I don't want her to shield anything from me.

It's bad enough that I don't know her name or how to reach her after tonight.

"Don't cover yourself," I hiss. "I want to see it all. I need to see it all."

Her breath hitches as the resistance fades and I drop her hands.

I can't stop myself when I lean forward and taste the spot between her tits. I run the tip of my tongue over the soft skin before I seek out her left nipple. I roll it in my fingers first, plumping it even more.

I glance at her face. Her eyes are heavy-lidded. I know she's craving my body the same way I'm craving hers.

I close my lips around her nipple and lightly flick my tongue over the hard, tight point.

Her hands fall to my hair, fingers twisting in the strands, guiding me closer to her.

I suck lightly as my hand moves to cup her right breast. I squeeze before I pinch the nipple hard just as my teeth close around the other.

She squeaks. "Oh, please."

Please take me. Please make me feel. Please fuck me.

I don't care if her plea is for one or all, I'll give her everything she needs.

CHAPTER SEVEN

LINNY

I'M ONLY WEARING my panties now.

The hideous tulle skirt is behind him on the floor. He slid it off me with care even though I was squirming in anticipation the entire time.

I wanted his eyes on me, his hands, his lips; all of him.

His gaze is pinned to the front of my white lace panties.

"Take them off, angel."

I've never stripped naked in front of a man before.

In the past, whenever I've known that sex was about to happen, I've crawled into bed under the shadow of darkness.

"Why don't you take off your…" My words trail when his hands land on the waistband of his boxer briefs. He slips them down to his knees and then further, kicking them aside.

I stare at him, all of him.

"Your turn." He grabs his thick cock, stroking himself while I watch each leisurely movement.

My gaze finds his and my breath catches. I glide my hands down my body until I feel the edge of the lace.

I lower my panties slowly with his eyes following each movement I make. It feels intimate in a way that makes my heart skip a beat.

A groan escapes him when the lace skims my thighs and I push the panties off, stepping out of them carefully before I brush them aside with a sweep of my foot.

"You're wet." The deep timbre of his voice makes me ache. "Show me how wet you are."

I'm so wet that you can fuck me right here, right now.

I don't say the words, even though I want to scream them at him.

His gaze scans my body. "I know you're slick. I want to see. Touch yourself and show me."

"Touch me," I whisper the only two words I can manage.

His eyes focus on my mouth before they dart to my pussy. "Show me, angel. Do it now."

I do. I drop my hand and run my fingertips over my aching cleft stopping to rub my clit.

"Don't." His hand is on my wrist halting my fingers in place. "Save that for tomorrow when you're thinking about me fucking you."

He raises my hand to his mouth and brushes his tongue against my fingertips. Electricity radiates through me.

"You taste as sweet as I imagined." His voice is low and measured.

He leans forward to press a soft kiss to my lips, his hand wrapping around the back of my neck.

"I want to take my time, and I will, but right now I need to be inside you." His hand drops to my pussy as he glides two thick fingers over my folds.

I cry out when he pushes them inside of me. It's a burst of pain wrapped in pleasure.

"You're going to make me come so hard," he says in a whisper.

His words are only urging me closer to the edge. I could orgasm just from listening to this man talk about wanting to fuck me.

I whimper when he slides his fingers out. "West."

He holds my hands in his and starts walking backward. "You're so fucking gorgeous. I can't take my eyes off of you."

I don't want him to.

I want to sear into my memory the way he's looking at me right now.

As we reach an open doorway, he skims the wall inside with his hand. A tall lamp comes on in the corner, filling the bedroom with warm, muted light.

I hesitate. I've never made love with the lights on.

"Don't be shy." His tone is soft. "You're a stunning woman with the sexiest body I've ever seen."

I bite back a smile. Tonight isn't about calling this stranger out on whether he's whispering words that are grounded in truth or not. I came to his hotel suite for an experience I know I'll never forget.

I step inside the doorway. His hand drops mine and he starts across the room. One word leaves his lips. "Condom."

It's a simple word; a necessary word, but it's laced with the promise of what's about to happen.

He tugs a foil packet from the pocket of a pair of pants that are draped over the back of a chair. He rips it open, letting the wrapper fall to the carpeted floor before he sheathes himself with ease.

"Come, angel."

I cross the room to where he is, my body shaking in anticipation.

His lips brush against mine in a fevered kiss as he pulls me onto the bed.

"Jesus," he hisses out when I reach down to wrap my hand around his cock. "Something tells me I'm going to remember this night forever."

Before I can think, he's on top of me, his large frame hovering over me.

I stare into his eyes. "I'll remember it too."

"You're fucking right you will," he says hoarsely. "This is just the beginning. You're mine until the sun comes up."

He eases into me slowly, taking his time.

My hips buck in a need to feel more. There are a million things I want to say, but nothing falls from my lips but a breathy moan.

He moves slowly, giving me time to adjust to his size. When I slide my hands down his back, he groans loudly.

His eyes lock on mine and as much as I want to close my eyes to hide what I'm feeling I don't.

I stare at him as he ups the pace and pumps into me with even, steady strokes.

I've never felt this full. It's never been so good. I race closer to the edge, letting out a low moan.

"Ah, fuck, that sound," he growls into the flesh of my neck before his teeth find my shoulder.

He bites my skin and I'm lost to it all.

Each thrust is harder. Every groan he makes is more intense. My pussy tightens as I near the edge. I try to open my mouth to say something, anything but only my breath escapes as I come.

His release follows with a carnal moan from deep within him that pushes me straight into another climax.

CHAPTER EIGHT

LINNY – 8 WEEKS LATER

I REPEAT BACK what Harmony just said to me. There's no way I heard her correctly. "Kendra is pregnant, and she thinks it happened on their wedding night?"

"Why are you acting like this is the first you've heard of it?"

I lock eyes with her across the table. "Because it is. When did you find out?"

She drops her gaze to her lap. "Two days ago. She called Priscilla right before she called me. I'm sorry, Linny. I thought you knew."

I don't know why I'm surprised that Kendra didn't reach out to share her good news with me.

I've been the odd woman out for years. The three of them have a lot in common. It was evident the day Kendra walked down the aisle five weeks ago in Atlanta.

Harmony's son was the ring bearer, and Priscilla's daughters were the flower girls. They spent hours with Kendra after the mid-day rehearsal the day before the ceremony. I spent that time alone in my hotel room answering work emails.

I went to Atlanta solo because I couldn't bear the thought of asking any of the men I know to accompany me on a weekend trip.

Any man other than West, that is.

It's been almost two months since I was in his hotel suite in Vegas, but I admit that he's invaded my thoughts on a regular basis.

Often, it's at night when I'm in bed.

My mind wanders to the memory of the sound of his voice, and how his hands felt on my body.

After we had sex, he got up to dispose of the condom in the washroom. When he came back to bed, he held me tightly whispering gentle words about how he was going to lick my pussy until I couldn't take it anymore before he fucked me again.

We both drifted off to sleep before that could happen. When I woke up the next morning, I realized that I needed to be at the airport less than two hours later for my flight to New York, so I got dressed and raced out of his room without waking him.

I spent the bulk of the flight ignoring questions from Harmony and Priscilla about where I'd been all night.

I didn't tell them, or anyone else that I was with a gorgeous stranger.

"Don't be upset," Harmony says as she pierces her fork into a piece of one of the blueberry pancakes on her plate. "Kendra had a field trip the day she called to tell me about the baby. She probably didn't have time to make three calls. "

I smile across the table at her when I see the concern in her eyes. Harmony has always been the peacemaker of our group. She took on the job of keeping everyone in our friendship foursome happy even though no one asked her to.

"I'm not upset," I say honestly. "I'm excited for Kendra. I know she's eager to be a mom."

"She's already talking about setting up a nursery." She heaves a sigh. "I told her to wait until she hits her second trimester, but she's out looking at cribs with Danny today."

I glance at my phone when it chimes with a new text message. Before I can pick it up, Harmony's hand is on mine. "It's work, isn't it?"

I read the brief message from my dad. "I have a lot on my plate."

"It's Saturday," she points out with a wave of the fork in her hand in my direction. "The only thing on your plate is one poached egg, a piece of bacon and a half-eaten piece of toast."

I look down at the breakfast special I ordered but barely touched. "I have to go into the office today."

Harmony's gaze darts around the interior of the diner we're in. When she called me last night to tell me she'd be in the city today, I told her to meet me for brunch at Crispy Biscuit. It's a favorite of mine. I come here every Saturday morning. "That's bullshit."

"It's my life." I sigh.

"That's why you're dressed like that?"

I give the black pants and white blouse I'm wearing a once-over. Harmony opted for a more relaxed look. She's wearing jeans and a lightweight pink sweater.

"What's wrong with how I'm dressed?" I smile.

"It's not exactly hot man bait." She rolls her eyes. "Speaking of hot men…are you seeing anyone? Or fucking anyone? Are you doing anything with any good-looking men?"

I rub my hand over my mouth to hide the wide grin on my lips. "I'm busy with work."

"I take that to mean you haven't seen a cock in a while." Her brows perk. "Maybe since Vegas? I know you hooked up with that hot-as-hell stripper."

"I didn't." I look her straight in the eye. "Nothing happened between us."

She studies my face. "You came back to the room with your tank top inside out, so if you didn't do the stripper, you picked up a random."

I shrug off her words. "I prefer to live in the present."

"Fine," she huffs. "Presently your pussy is lonely."

I glance around the diner, trying to contain my laugh. "I want to come back here for brunch next week so let's change the subject before they toss us out."

That lures a smile to her lips. "You could use some action."

"As much as I'd like to talk about my sex life all day, I have just enough time to hear about what's happening in your life." I tap the face of my watch. "Give it to me in thirty seconds or less."

"Thirty seconds or less?" She tosses my words back with a lift of her brow. "Things are good at work. They're perfect at home. I'm living my dream."

I push back from the table, fishing in my purse for my wallet. "Today is my treat, right? You picked up the tab last time?"

Last time was the week before Kendra's wedding when Harmony and I went to lunch before we tackled shopping for a joint wedding gift.

She nods. "Tell David that I think he should cut you a break and give you a weekend off."

I toss some money on the table before I shoulder my bag. "I'll tell my dad you said hi and that you miss him."

"That's not quite the same, but fine," she says with a smile. "I do miss him. He was the biggest fan of our volleyball team during senior year."

He was. My dad never missed a game. He cheered Harmony and I on with everything he had. It meant a lot to her since her dad died before her tenth birthday.

I lean down to give her a hug. "Text me this week if anything exciting happens."

She pats my back. "Promise me you won't work too hard."

I can't promise that. I need to work as hard as I can if I'm going to take over as CEO of Faye & Sons once my dad retires next year.

I have a lot to prove to him, and I'll take advantage of every opportunity I can to show him that I'm the woman for the job.

———

"WHY IS SHE HERE?" My stepbrother, Mitchell, looks across the conference table at my dad as I walk in. "Isn't she knee deep in the campaign for that Walters woman?"

"Ivy Marlow-Walker?" I smile at my dad just as he's about to open his mouth to respond. "She owns a multi-million dollar jewelry design business, Mitchell. She's an important client. Actually, every client we have is important which is why I make it a point to research all of them, even if I'm not working directly with them."

My dad beams at my words, his green eyes lighting up.

"Whatever, Linny." Mitchell skims his hand over his short blond hair. "We aren't here to talk about rings and bracelets."

We're here on a Saturday to discuss a new major client who reached out to our firm last week.

"I asked Linny to join us." My dad stands as I approach him. "I want all hands on deck on this one."

Mitchell rolls his blue eyes.

I'm used to it. I'm used to everything about him since we met ten years ago when my dad started dating his mom.

Back then, Mitchell was a lost twenty-year-old. He had a high school diploma and no direction. My dad's influence was enough to persuade Mitchell to go to college to study advertising.

I focused on a marketing degree and ever since we've been in a silent battle to earn a seat behind the desk in my dad's office once he celebrates his sixty-fifth birthday next year and jets off to retirement in Florida with my stepmom, Diane.

My dad takes me into his arms for a quick hug. "Thanks for coming, sweetheart."

"I wouldn't miss this for the world, Dad." I drop my purse on the table and settle into one of the chairs.

"Me either, Dad," Mitchell drawls. He conveniently refers to my dad that way only when it benefits him. The rest of the time he calls him Dave.

"Alright, team. Let's get to work," my dad says, taking the seat at the head of the table.

We're far from a team, but I'll play nice if it's good for the company since I know that one day soon, Mitchell Bilton will be answering to me and me alone.

CHAPTER NINE

JEREMY

"I'M TAPPING OUT, ROCCO." I rest my hands on my knees. My leg muscles are on fire. "For fuck's sake you win, alright? You win. Dinner is on me."

Rocco turns to look at me.

He's as worn out as I am, but he was determined to win our bet.

We made the wager right before we started our run through Central Park. Whoever quit first had to cover the cost of dinner tonight. I knew before we crossed the street in front of his apartment that I'd be the one pulling my wallet out at the end of our meal.

"We're eating at Nova. It's that place in Greenwich Village. You're heard of it, right?" He lifts a hand to wipe away the sweat pouring down his face and onto his bare chest. "I'm ordering the most expensive dish on the menu."

"You're an asshole." I laugh. "If I would have won, we'd be eating a BLT and fries at Crispy Biscuit."

"You order that every time we meet there for lunch." His hands drop to his hips right above where his black shorts are sitting.

I stand straight and suck in a few deep breaths. "We're not going to Nova. It takes weeks to get a reservation. Pick another place."

"We have a reservation for tonight." He approaches me, his gaze drifting over my shoulder.

"You made a reservation?" I huff out a laugh. "When?"

"Four days ago when you invited yourself along for my Saturday afternoon run and told me that you could beat me in distance."

"Cocky bastard." I rub my hand over the back of my neck. "What time are we doing this?"

"Eight." He tilts his chin up. "You down for double or nothing?"

I cock a brow. "Now?"

"Right now."

We've been tossing bets back and forth since he signed on as a partner in my business. I've yet to turn one down. "I'm in."

"If I win, we drink a bottle of their most expensive wine with dinner. If you win, we'll go to Crispy Biscuit."

"I'll win. Tell me what I need to do."

"Check that tracker app on your phone." He points at the phone that's strapped to my bicep. "If it's turned on, I'll be sipping the best chardonnay money can buy tonight. If it's turned off, you'll get that bacon, lettuce and tomato sandwich you want."

"It's a bet and I win," I announce with a grin. "I deleted that fucking app two days ago."

His gaze jumps over my shoulder again. "Check your phone, Jeremy."

I tug open the strap on my arm and release my phone. "Unless you know something I don't, there's no way in hell you're winning this bet."

"Mr. Weston?"

I curse under my breath when I hear the voice behind me. It's Blythe, my assistant.

"Oh, Mr. Jones." She brushes past me to extend her hand to Rocco. "You're looking…well."

Rocco takes her hand in his. "It's Blythe, right?"

She giggles at that even though she's married and at least three decades older than him. "You remembered."

"How could I forget you?" he asks with a straight face. He's dropped by my office twice and both times Blythe practically tripped over her own feet rushing to get him a cup of coffee made exactly the way he likes.

"Tell me this is a coincidence, Blythe." I look at her purple shorts and pink butterfly-patterned blouse. "Thank you for never wearing that to the office."

She bats a hand over my shoulder. "You've been ignoring my calls, Jeremy."

"It's Saturday." I skim my fingers over my phone's screen. I know I'll find that damn app back on my phone. Blythe and I have been doing a back-and-forth dance for the past month. She installs it on my phone to track where I am. I delete the app and change my phone's password.

She guesses the new password and we start the cycle all over again.

"Shit," I say under my breath when I spot the app. "When the hell did you have your hands on my phone during the past two days?"

She shrugs as she watches me delete it again. "Yesterday. You ran to the break room to get me a coffee."

"He gets you coffee?" Rocco's voice draws Blythe's attention back to him.

I shoot him a look. "I was headed in that direction."

"I appreciate it." Blythe pats my cheek before she swipes her palm across the front of her blouse. "You're a little sweaty."

I cup my jaw. I want to get out of here and home to a cool shower. "Why did you chase me down today? The office is closed. You're supposed to be enjoying your day off with Harve."

"Harve is having a nap." Brushing a strand of her gray hair behind her ear, she glances up at Rocco. "My hubby doesn't have the same stamina as a young fellow like you."

He leans in close to her. "When he wakes up tell him what a lucky man he is to have you."

Her mouth lifts in a broad smile. "I'll be sure to tell him you said that."

"Blythe." I snap my fingers. "Over here. Why the hell did you track me down?"

She nods her head. "Oh, right. I left an invitation on your desk yesterday. I know you opened it. You were supposed to RSVP by noon today."

I look at my phone's screen. It's twelve-thirty. "You raced out here to ask if I'd be willing to have dinner with your best friend's niece tomorrow night?"

"She's perfect for you, Jeremy. "She takes a step back to look over my dark blue running shorts and matching T-shirt. "Clean yourself up and shave. She likes boys who are clean-shaven."

Rocco chuckles.

I don't glance in his direction. I keep my gaze squarely on my assistant. "Lindsay is a lovely woman, Blythe, but…"

"But nothing," she interrupts. "You're a perfect match.

You're both single. I saw the sparks that were flying between you two when she came to visit me at the office last week."

There wasn't a spark in sight; at least not on my end.

"I'm interested in someone else. It's going to be a no, Blythe."

She studies my face carefully. "Why have I not met this woman you're interested in?"

Because I don't know who the fuck she is.

I spent a few hours with her in a hotel room in Vegas two months ago and I can't stop thinking about her.

I've tried.

Jesus, have I tried.

I've taken women to dinner. I've gone home with them, and every single fucking time, I don't end up in bed. Instead, I retell the story of the gorgeous green-eyed woman in the pink tutu I met on my way to Vegas and how she disappeared before I woke up.

It still haunts me that I only got a taste. If I would have kept my goddamn eyes open that night I would have had more time with her.

For the rest of my life, I'm going to regret falling asleep that night.

Rocco clears his throat. He's heard me complain about Blythe a handful of times the past few months including last week when I told him she put that tracker app on my phone.

He knows she oversteps, but he's well aware of what an asset she is to me. She's one of the few people in this world that I trust.

"I'm heading up Central Park South." Rocco offers his arm to Blythe. "Can I walk you somewhere?"

She grabs his bicep, wrapping her hand around it. "I'm ready. Let's go."

"You live in the opposite direction, Blythe," I point out.

"I know." She winks at me. "We're going to take the scenic route."

I shake my head as I watch them walk away. Hundreds of people are in the park on this warm summer afternoon, but my gaze is only drawn to women with shoulder-length brown hair.

I have no idea if the woman I spent the night with in Las Vegas lives in Manhattan, but that hasn't stopped me from scanning the face of every brunette I've seen since that night.

I may never lay eyes on her again, but it sure as hell doesn't hurt to look.

CHAPTER TEN

LINNY

I GLANCE down at my phone and the text message that just arrived.

Harmony: *I told you he was hot.*

I hate when she's right, but I can't deny that the man she set me up with is good-looking.

This is the third time in the past year that Harmony has arranged a date for me. The first two times I didn't make it to the dessert course before I called it a night.

I'm enjoying a delicious slice of cheesecake with fresh blueberries at the moment, so Roland Elgar is faring better than any of the other men Harmony thought would be perfect for me.

"It doesn't bother me if you check your phone, Linny." Roland smiles as he finishes the last bite of the strawberry napoleon he ordered. "My work follows me out of the office too."

He's a professor of economics at NYU. He owns a townhouse in Brooklyn and spends his Sunday afternoons having dinner with his brother who happens to teach at the same school as Harmony.

It was during one of those dinners a few weeks ago that Harmony met Roland. They kept in touch, she mentioned me to him, and this afternoon she texted me to see if I was free for dinner.

I know she arranged it because she felt sorry for me after our brunch earlier. I told her as much in my text reply, but she responded almost instantly that he was the one who reached out to her today to see if I was available.

I didn't believe her but since I had nothing on my agenda, and I love the food here at Nova, I told her I'd meet him after I did a quick search for him online.

His bio picture on the New York University website doesn't do him justice. His black hair is mussed from the wind outside. His green eyes are a shade darker than mine. He's dressed in a navy blue suit with a white shirt and purple tie.

We both lean back when the server approaches to remove our dessert plates. "Can I get either of you an after dinner drink?"

I look to Roland for guidance. I'm not about to invite him back to my place, and if he offers up the promise of a nightcap at his townhouse, I'll turn him down. Our date will be over if we decline the drink offer.

"I'll have a brandy." Roland smiles at me. "How about you?"

I look around the crowded restaurant. I like the ambiance and since I'm enjoying myself, I nod. "I'll have the same."

He waits until the server leaves before he clears his throat. "I realize that our first date hasn't officially ended yet, but I'm about to ask you for a second."

My gaze drifts over his shoulder. I catch sight of two men sitting at a table across the restaurant. The man facing me is attractive but it's the man who has his back to me that grabs my attention.

He's wearing a suit jacket that's the same shade of gray as the one West had on when we met on the airplane. He also has the same hair color as West. A lot of men in this city do. I've taken notice since I got back from Vegas.

"I can wait to ask until you've had a day or two to decide if you're interested." Roland chuckles. "Obviously, I'm interested in you."

I should be interested in him too. He's a nice guy with no apparent baggage. That's a rarity in this city, but for some reason, I'm not feeling any butterflies in my stomach at the prospect of another date.

"Roland?" A man's voice draws my attention to the right. "What the hell are you doing here?"

Roland pushes back from the table and is on his feet in an instant. Before he can say anything, he's being tugged into the arms of a tall man wearing a chef's jacket.

They exchange a friendly hug. When they step apart, Roland smiles at the chef. "Tyler. Damn, man, it's been forever."

Tyler? As in Chef Tyler Monroe?

I'm not a foodie, but I know enough about the Manhattan restaurant scene to realize that Tyler Monroe is a wizard in the kitchen. He's one of the most celebrated chefs in this city.

"It's been at least two years, Roland." Tyler's gaze falls to where I'm still seated. He extends his hand. "I'm sorry. I'm normally not this rude. I'm Tyler."

"You're not rude," I say, sliding to my feet and taking his hand in mine. "I'm Linny."

"Are you two…" Tyler's words trail as he shoots Roland a look.

"This is our first date." Roland pats Tyler's shoulder. "I brought her here to impress her."

I smile at that. "It worked. The food is incredible."

Tyler's brows shoot up. "I would have prepared something special off menu if I knew Roland was having dinner with a woman with such good taste in food and…"

"Men?" Roland interrupts.

"Wine." Tyler points at the empty bottle of merlot on the table. "You must have a discerning palate, Linny. From what I remember, cheap beer was Roland's drink of choice."

I laugh at the obvious jab.

"If that was supposed to be an insult, I'm not going to complain." Roland's voice lowers. "Say whatever the hell you want about me if it brings a smile to Linny's beautiful face."

I may agree to that second date after all.

"I was on my way to say hello to one of my suppliers." Tyler motions to the table where the two men I noticed earlier are sitting. "My work is never done."

"We won't keep you." Roland rests his hand on the back of his chair. "It was good to see you. Give me a call sometime. We need to catch up."

"I'm previewing the fall tasting menu on Friday night at eight o'clock. It's a private event. You two are more than welcome to join us."

Roland's mouth curls into a smile. "I'm in. How about you, Linny? Is it a date?"

If I had any doubt about accepting a second date invitation, it's been washed away by the promise of delicious food and wine. "I'll be here."

"I'll see you both then." Tyler squeezes Roland's shoulder. "It was great to see you old friend and really good to meet you, Linny."

"It was good to meet you too," I reply, but he's already making his way across the crowded dining room.

The server approaches with two brandy snifters in his hands. Roland reaches for the back of my chair and motions for me to sit.

Once we're both settled in, he toasts to our upcoming date on Friday night.

I raise my glass and clink it against his.

Maybe Harmony did get it right this time. Only time will tell.

CHAPTER ELEVEN

JEREMY

"WHEN'S THE last time you suited up?" I tilt my chin up.

Rocco looks down at the jeans, white T-shirt and black jacket he's wearing before he points a finger at my tailored gray suit. "I'm touched that you pulled out one of your three thousand dollar suits to take me to dinner."

I straighten the cuff of my jacket. "I'm thinking of hitting up a club after this. You're welcome to tag along."

He pauses before he smiles. "Are you meeting the woman you told Blythe about?"

I fucking wish I was. I shake my head.

"You were letting Blythe down easy when you said you were interested in someone else?" He strokes his chin. "I take it the friend's niece isn't your type."

"You could say that."

"So you're headed to the club to find your type?" He narrows his gaze. "I'll let you handle that without a wingman. It's a pass for me."

"We just talked shop over dinner. A break from work won't kill you."

Beneath the bet and time spent together running this afternoon, this evening was always designed to be a business meeting. Rocco's been itching for an update on the vanilla vodka's launch. I just spent the past two hours filling him in on every detail.

He wasn't kidding when he said he was going to order the most expensive entrée on the menu. He did. He washed it back with a bottle of cabernet recommended by our server.

It's worth every dime now that I'm watching Tyler Monroe make his way to our table. He's the owner of Nova and the head chef. He also agreed to sell Rizon vodka exclusively to his diners three months ago.

I do a double take when I catch the profile of a woman sitting at a table with a dark-haired guy in a blue suit. I swear to fuck she looks like my Vegas angel.

Before I can get a better look at her, Tyler is next to me with his hand resting on my shoulder.

"Jeremy, it's good to see you."

I nod as I try to steal another look at the woman who just made my heart race. I curse to myself when I realize that the guy she's with is blocking my line of sight.

"You too, Tyler," I offer with a grin. "This is Rocco Jones, my business partner."

Rocco extends his hand to the chef who takes it for a quick shake. "It's great to meet you, Tyler."

"How was your dinner?" Tyler crosses his arms over his chest.

Rocco looks down at his empty plate. "There's your answer. Nova never disappoints."

A smile creeps over Tyler's mouth as he rakes a hand through his brown hair. "That's good to hear."

"How's Cadence and Firi?" I ask about his family because I know Tyler. Those two people are his life. Nova is his passion. He's determined to make the restaurant the top in Manhattan, but he'd push it aside in an instant for the woman he loves and their son.

"They're great, Jeremy. Thanks for asking," he answers, holding my gaze.

The pull I feel to turn around to try to get another look at the brunette is strong, but I stick to script. The launch of the vanilla vodka is less than two months away and I need all the exposure I can get.

I'll chat up Tyler for a few minutes, excuse myself, and then head over to the table where the drop-dead gorgeous woman is sitting.

"I dropped off a sample bottle of our new product last week." I shoot a look at the bar manager, Leo. I hand delivered a bottle to him with the understanding that he'd see to it that Tyler not only got a taste but a sterling recommendation from him. I could have left that job to our Brand Manager, but I didn't want to risk the chance that Leo would turn him down. Leo's words are what got Rizon vodka into Nova. I'm trusting that he's worked his magic again.

"Leo loves it." Tyler turns his head toward the bar. "It's the best vanilla vodka I've tasted. Leo has my go-ahead to stock it once it's released."

I make a mental note to thank Leo before I leave. "I'll touch base with him and work out the details."

"Sounds good." Tyler motions for a server. "I'll get these plates cleared. You two interested in dessert?"

I'm interested in the brunette who I swear looks like the angel I met in Vegas. I glance back over my shoulder, but she's gone. The guy she was having dinner with is nowhere to be found either.

Fuck.

"I'm not going to turn down dessert." Rocco laughs. "Are you in, Jeremy, or are you in a hurry to take off?"

"I'm in." I look at my watch not caring about the time.

Once I leave here, I'll skip the club and go to my office until I can't focus anymore. After that, I'll head home and catch a few hours of sleep before I face Sunday head-on.

It's the only day that work is off the table.

"Are you two busy on Friday?" Tyler asks with a quirk of his brow. "I'm having a private party. It's a preview of the fall tasting menu."

Rocco glances at me before he turns to Tyler. "I wouldn't miss the chance to attend that."

"It's at eight." Tyler looks at the entrance of the restaurant where a group of people just arrived. "I need to run, but feel free to bring a guest each."

Rocco pushes to his feet. "It's been a pleasure, Chef."

I stand too and extend my hand to Tyler. "We'll see you on Friday."

"Friday it is," Tyler says as he takes my hand in his for a shake. "I've invited half of Manhattan, so I'm sure you'll both see a few familiar faces."

The only face I'm interested in seeing is the woman who was eating dinner just a few tables away from me.

Rocco and I watch Tyler move fluidly through the crowded dining room toward the kitchen.

"Sit down, Jeremy." Rocco lowers himself back into his chair. "I'm not leaving here without dessert."

"I need to take care of something." I rest my hands on the back of my chair. "Give me five minutes."

"Take your time." He touches the base of his empty wine glass. "I'll order another bottle of cabernet while I wait."

I huff out a laugh. "Order a glass of Rizon vodka."

He tugs his phone from his jacket pocket when it chimes. "I'll order two since I know you won't turn down a chance to sample your product."

I don't say another word as Rocco's fingers skim over the screen of his phone. Instead, I turn and head straight toward our server.

"What is it, sir?" he nervously asks when I near where he's standing close to the entrance to the kitchen. "Chef Monroe told me about your complimentary dessert. I'll bring it out as soon as it's ready."

"Sure." I lean in closer to him, lowering my voice. "A couple just left that table. I'm wondering if you served them."

"Which table?" He eyes the area behind me.

I turn back to see that the table is now occupied by two young women. I raise my hand in the air and point directly at them. "It's that table. There was a woman with brown hair and a man in a blue suit sitting there a few minutes ago."

He nods vigorously. "Oh, right. Yes. I took care of their needs."

I shake my head at his awkward choice of words. "You didn't catch their names, did you?"

His expression morphs into confusion. "Why? I'm only supposed to introduce myself to the guests. It's up to them if they introduce themselves to me."

"I take it that means no?"

"No," he answers back.

"Did he pay with a credit card?" I have no right to ask this kid anything, but curiosity is driving me. If he gives me a name, I can track down the couple and see for myself if she was indeed the woman I met two months ago.

"Cash." He shakes his head from side-to-side. "Even if he did pay by credit card, it's not like I could tell you his name. Privacy laws and all."

"Understood." I reach into the inner pocket of my suit jacket and pull out my wallet. I thumb through it before I slide out a hundred dollar bill. "I'll tip you at the table, but here's something extra for your trouble."

His gaze falls to the bill before he scoops it up in his palm. "Thanks, Jeremy."

Seeing as how I never introduced myself to him, I raise both brows. "How do you know my name?"

"Your friend, Rocco, called you Jeremy when I dropped off your appetizers." He gestures in the direction Rocco is sitting.

"Did the black-haired man happen to mention the beautiful brunette's name?"

He furrows his brow while his thumb slides over the folded bill in his palm. "I can't recall."

For fuck's sake. I'm being taken for hundreds because of my irrational need to know the name of a woman who may not even be the angel I spent the night with in Vegas.

I hand over another hundred because I'm already in too deep to bow out now.

"I didn't catch her name, but his is Roland."

"Roland," I repeat back.

"I'm glad I could be of service, " he adds as he gazes down at my money.

I almost reach forward to grab it from his greasy hand. "You were no help at all."

"I'll check on that dessert for you, Jeremy."

I shoot him a look before he walks into the kitchen leaving me with the first name of a man I already dislike. *Roland* may be headed home with the woman who has been haunting my every dream for the past eight weeks.

If he is, he's the luckiest son-of-a-bitch on the planet.

CHAPTER TWELVE

LINNY

"NO, MITCHELL, THAT'S WRONG." I shake my head. "The client's name is Trent Morrison, not Trent Morris. Get it together before our meeting."

"Our meeting?" Mitchell's blond brows pinch together. "Since when it is *our* meeting? I thought Dave was giving me the reins on this one."

I move to close his office door so the entire floor doesn't hear us disagreeing again. They already got an earful this morning when Mitchell stormed into my office to ask me why I'd sent a bouquet of flowers to one of our long-term clients who recently had surgery.

Mitchell has been her primary point of contact since she signed on with our firm three years ago, but I knew he wouldn't reach out after finding out that she had canceled her meeting with him today because she was in the hospital recovering from an emergency appendectomy a few days ago.

He was caught off guard when she called to thank him for

the lavish bouquet. By the time he stormed into my office, he was livid that I hadn't informed him that flowers had been sent to her along with a card with our firm's best wishes.

It wasn't my fault that he sounded like a fool as he sputtered his way through the conversation not even aware that she'd gone under the knife.

He sounded just as incompetent when I was passing by his office a few minutes ago and heard him telling his assistant, Hal, that he needed a pot of coffee ready for his three o'clock meeting with *Trent Morris*.

Trent Morrison is the brand manager for a vodka company. He's the reason I was called into the office on Saturday to meet with my dad and Mitchell.

I pitched my ideas before listening to Mitchell toss out a few of his tricd and true standards including a television commercial and a billboard in Times Square.

I'm not as prepared for this meeting as I want to be. The only research I've done is looking through Trent Morrison's recent social media posts.

I intended to spend yesterday studying the company's history and past advertising campaigns, but that didn't happen.

Ivy Marlow-Walker, the owner of Whispers of Grace, asked me to go over some of the proofs from a photo shoot I arranged last week. Since I'm the one who suggested we hire a photographer to capture new images of Ivy's latest jewelry designs, I couldn't refuse, even though it was Sunday.

After we finished for the day, I had dinner at her apartment with her and her family.

In terms of work, it was a great investment of my time, but it was more than that. It was a chance to get to know her husband and kids.

A soft knock at the door draws Mitchell to his feet. "Answer the door, Linny."

I'm tempted to tell him to do it, but I'm less than a foot away from it, so I swing open the door.

"It's not often that I find you two together." My dad brushes a hand over his bald head. "Nothing warms my heart more than to see you working side-by-side."

Mitchell clears his throat behind me. "Linny was just telling me that she'll be sitting in on the meeting with Trent Morrison."

His tongue lingers on the last syllable, making a note to pronounce it correctly.

"I've prepared a few more ideas for us to pitch." I ignore my stepbrother's attempt to undermine my role in the meeting.

My dad nods. "You're always coming up with something new and fresh, Linny."

I'd feel better accepting the compliment if I actually had more ideas to present to Mr. Morrison. I have just over an hour to brainstorm though so as soon as I can break free of Mitchell's office, I'll hunker down in mine with my assistant.

"It's my job," I say as I toss Mitchell a glance.

"You look beautiful as always today." My dad leans forward to kiss my cheek.

I gaze down at the red pencil skirt and black blouse I'm wearing. I pulled my hair back into a tight knot at the base of my neck before I applied my makeup this morning. I skipped my contact lenses for a pair of black-rimmed eyeglasses. After slipping on strappy black heels, I was out the door and at the office before my nine a.m. start time.

"The glasses make you look smarter," Mitchell calls from behind me.

I turn so I'm facing him directly with my back to my dad.

I lift my middle finger and silently mouth the words, "*Fuck you.*"

The smug grin on his face morphs into a scowl.

"I'll see you at three, Mitchell," I say cheerfully. "I overheard you asking Hal to make coffee for the meeting, but Mr. Morrison prefers a particular green tea that is only sold at a café on Fifth Avenue. I'll call there myself and have it delivered piping hot."

"It's all about attention to detail." My dad squeezes my shoulder. "You always know exactly what our clients want."

I know that Trent Morrison stops at that café regularly to get a large green tea brewed at precisely one hundred and seventy-five degrees.

He's documented it enough times on social media that anyone who follows his account would think he's getting paid to promote their product.

I turn back to my dad. "I've got to get back to my office, but I'll see you at the meeting."

His gaze volleys between Mitchell and me. I know that look. He's contemplating not only his future but my jerk of a stepbrother's and mine too.

That's why I need to shine at this meeting. It's a chance to show my dad that I'm the best choice when he appoints a new CEO.

CHAPTER THIRTEEN

JEREMY

"TODAY?" I glance down at the watch on my wrist. "You booked that meeting for today?"

Trent Morrison, the Brand Manager for Rizon, gives me a curt nod. "You said to set it up as soon as possible. I reached out to David last week and he blocked out two hours at three o'clock today."

"As in forty-five minutes from now?"

I know he can hear the irritation in my voice. I don't fucking care. I've had one issue after another thrown at me since I got to my office this morning. Having to abandon the fires that are already burning so I can trek across town to sit down with David Faye and his team isn't part of my plan.

"You can't reschedule?" I ask with a brisk brush of my hand in the air. "I'm up to my neck in bullshit today. Make it another day this week."

"No can do," he says cheerfully. "Faye is booked up solid

for the next six weeks. You don't want to know what I had to do to get this meeting."

He's right. I don't want to know. I did tell him in no uncertain terms to get us some time over at Faye's office and he delivered that.

It's impressive given the tight time frame I gave him to make it happen.

I brought Trent on board a year ago when our last Brand Manager jumped ship and took on a prominent role at Estey Vodka. They're our biggest competitor and slowly but surely they've been plucking away all of my valued employees, leaving me with no choice but to replace them with new hires.

Trent claims his strong suit is social media engagement. He's offered no proof of that yet and with the vanilla vodka launch looming, I want more hands on deck, which is why I told him to call David Faye.

David's name is gold in New York advertising. My first choice was Rocco's brother, Nash. He's done good work for me in the past but he just landed a high-profile tech client. He's focused on the promotional campaign for the worldwide launch of a new smartphone and doesn't have time to devote to Rizon.

My plan to build an in-house marketing team hasn't happened yet. I make a mental note to put that at the top of my priority list once our new vodka hits the market.

"I can handle it on my own." Trent makes himself at home by taking a seat in one of the chairs on the opposite side of my desk. "Send me over there by myself and I'll come back with a kick ass advertising plan in place."

Tension tightens my shoulders. "That's not an option."

His head pops up. There's no surprise in his expression.

He knows that I lack confidence in his abilities. I remind him often enough.

"You don't need to be there, Jeremy," he stresses as he adjusts the collar of his light blue suit jacket. Combined with his curly blond hair and freshly shaved jaw he looks like he just stepped off a college campus.

He's my age, but you'd never know that by looking at him.

"This launch is huge." He spreads his arms apart to reinforce his point. "We can't skip this meeting and if you're too tied down with other stuff, I'll take the lead."

"There's no way in hell I'm sending you over there on your own." I lean back in my chair. "I need to be there."

I also need to meet with my lead attorney in ten minutes. I told him to get his ass down to my office for two-thirty sharp. I can't blow him off.

I stand as a signal for Trent to leave. "I'll meet you there."

"We can ride over together in the company car."

"The company car?" I knit my brow. "We don't have a company car, Trent."

"We don't?" His gaze scans my face. "Blythe calls for the car whenever I need it."

"She what?" I fist my hands by my sides. "What kind of car is it?"

"Cadillac," he says confidently. "The driver's name is Con."

"As in I'm being conned into paying for your ass to get around Manhattan in a car?"

He laughs. "Conrad is the guy's name."

Conrad.

I scrub the back of my neck with my hand. "Get yourself a MetroCard. You can expense the cost. Your free ride is officially over."

"Seriously?" His brows shoot up. "You want me to take the subway today?"

"Unless you'd prefer to run." I point to my office door. "You need to be uptown in thirty-five minutes. Get moving."

"Unbelievable," he mutters under his breath as he opens the door and walks out.

"Blythe," I yell her name through the open doorway. "I need you in here now."

I watch as she lazily closes the distance from her desk to my office doorway. I wait until she's stepped over the threshold before I say another word.

"Shut the door behind you."

She gives it a push with her foot sending it slamming shut. "I pissed you off again, didn't I?"

I stare down at her. She's wearing a yellow dress with white polka dots. The woman has no shame when it comes to her wardrobe choices. "What's your grandson been up to lately?"

She looks at me. "Conrad?"

Nodding silently, I shrug into my black suit jacket.

"Oh, you know," she pauses. "Con is always doing a little of this and a little of that."

That's the main reason why I didn't hire him when he applied for a junior position in accounting a year ago. He may have finished college with a degree, but his head is in the clouds.

I turned him down, listened to Blythe bitch about it for a month and then forgot the guy even existed, until now.

"From what I hear he's doing a lot of driving for Rizon." With a sigh, I look toward the door. "That stops today."

"You know?" There's a hint of resignation in her voice. "You told me I could do whatever was necessary to keep things running smoothly. Con's an Uber driver. There are places our people need to be. It seemed like a great idea at the time."

"People?" I glance at the clock on my wall. My attorney should be outside my door in less than a minute if he's still as punctual as I remember. "I know about Trent. Who else was getting a free ride?"

Her gaze drops to the floor. "Me."

"You?"

She nods slowly. "I only did it a few times last winter when we were hit with those storms. I didn't think my arthritic knees would make it through the snow to the subway stop, so I called Con."

I should fire her, but I won't. I can't. I'm holding onto her until she decides she's done with the job.

"Trent's not getting in Con's Cadillac again." I cross my arms. "If you need him to drive you to work and back home, we can set something up. That arrangement only applies to you."

"Are you serious?" She reaches toward me but stops herself. "I thought you were going to fire me."

I contain a smile. "I should. No one else would get away with the shit you pull, Blythe."

"I'll behave," she lies.

I laugh. "You won't. Get back to your desk. My attorney should be out there looking for me by now."

"Thanks, boss." She grins. "I know you'll never admit it, but your heart is made of gold."

I drop my gaze to the floor.

She knows what to do. She leaves my office, softly shutting the door behind her as I ready myself before I face my attorney and an issue I've pushed to the side for far too long.

CHAPTER FOURTEEN

LINNY

I GAZE across the conference table at Trent Morrison. He rushed into the office at three o'clock sharp with his suit jacket in his hand and his tie hanging loosely around his neck.

He was muttering something about hating the subway and the asshole that took his car away.

I ignored all of that as I approached him at reception and introduced myself.

Before I could ask him if he needed a few minutes to compose himself, Mitchell appeared and took Trent's sweaty palm in his own for an overzealous handshake.

As the two men made their way down the long corridor to the conference room, I followed in silence.

I know from experience if Mitchell talks long enough he's bound to say something offensive.

He did when he introduced Trent as Trent Morris to my dad.

Trent jumped in to correct him with a scowl and an eye roll.

Thankfully, the sight of the large green tea I had delivered for him was enough to bring a smile back to Mr. Morrison's face.

"We can get started whenever you're ready, Trent." My dad taps the palm of his hand on the top of the wooden conference table. "We've got some ideas for the launch that we're looking forward to sharing with you."

Trent looks at my dad. "I take it you all sampled the product."

Out of the corner of my eye, I catch Mitchell nodding his head. "Thanks again for that bottle you sent over this morning, Trent. I poured a shot for almost everyone in the office. The consensus is that it's the best we've ever tasted."

Almost everyone?

The jerk didn't include me in his pre-meeting drinking party.

"I admit that I've been a fan of your traditional vodka for years," my dad says with a grin. "I'll be switching to this new one as soon as it hits store shelves."

Trent turns his attention to me. "What about you, Linny? What did you think of it?"

I feel Mitchell's gaze burning into me, but I ignore him and focus on Trent. "I wanted to wait for you to arrive before I took my first taste. I'd love if you'd join me in a toast to the future of Rizon."

"I'm up for that." He scans the room. "Where's the bottle?"

I'm already texting a message to Hal, Mitchell's assistant, asking him to bring the bottle to the conference room along with four shot glasses. His response is instant. He's on his way.

"It's arriving at any moment." I place my phone back on the table. "If we had some caviar to go with it I'd be in heaven. I wish that place on Amsterdam and Seventy-Eighth delivered."

"Mysa Caviar Bar?" Trent flashes me a wide smile. "You're a fan too?"

I've never been, but Trent is a regular. According to the pictures posted to his Instagram account, he's there at least once a week.

A soft knock at the door saves me from having to bluff my way through a conversation about Mysa.

Just as my dad pushes to his feet, Mitchell shouts, "Why the hell are you knocking? Just come in, Hal."

Fighting off a grin, I drop my gaze to my lap.

No one can ever accuse Mitchell of being a top-notch professional. I'm hopeful Trent is keeping a running tally of my performance versus my stepbrother's, so when we do land this account, I'll be the one spearheading it.

The door opens before my dad is halfway around the table. He stops in place as Mitchell hurriedly rises to his feet.

"You should always knock before you open a door."

My head shoots up at the sound of the masculine voice. It's not Hal's. This voice is deep, raspy and achingly familiar.

"Sorry to disappoint, but I'm not Hal." He adjusts his silver necktie. "I'm Jeremy Weston, the owner of Rizon Vodka."

Holy shit, it's him.

The man I slept with in Las Vegas is standing in the doorway.

He's as gorgeous as I remember.

Everything about him is insanely sexy right down to his dark brown eyes. He's surveying the room, taking in each face. When he reaches mine, he stops to stare.

"I didn't know you'd be joining us, Mr. Weston." My dad rushes toward him with his hand outstretched. "I'm David Faye."

"It's a pleasure, David." His mouth curves up in a smile as he glances at me again.

"I brought the vodka." Hal appears behind West with a wooden tray in his hands. "Should I get another glass?"

"Yes," Mitchell hisses as he pushes his hand into West's. "I'm Mitchell Bilton. I'll be taking the reins on this project, Mr. Weston. I can assure you that I'm going to make certain that every person in the Tri-State area knows about Rizon Vodka."

Since the launch is nationwide, I should be thrilled that Mitchell has put his foot in his mouth again, but I don't feel anything but shock at the sight of the man I spent the most memorable night of my life with.

"You arrived just in time for our toast." Mitchell takes the tray from Hal. "As I was telling Trent, Rizon vanilla is the best vodka I've ever sampled."

West doesn't acknowledge him at all. He stands in silence with his gaze pinned to me.

How is this real?

I never thought I'd see him again after our night in Vegas.

Mitchell places the tray on the table and starts pouring out shots. When he reaches the last glass, he holds the open bottle in his hand.

"Where is Hal?" he asks impatiently to no one in particular. "We need another glass."

West looks around the room before his gaze falls back on the glasses on the tray. "There are enough."

"We're one short." Mitchell points at everyone as if he's counting to himself. "Five people. Four shot glasses. We need another."

West rests both hands on the conference table and locks eyes with me. "You haven't changed your stance on day drinking have you?"

Shit.

Faye & Sons has a strict policy that prohibits anyone in the company from being romantically involved with a client. My dad put that in place after Mitchell fucked up. He literally fucked the wife of a major client. We lost the account, but my stepbrother managed to hold onto his job by his fingernails.

After that disaster, everyone who works at Faye & Sons had to sign an amendment to their employment contract that stated that they would be subject to significant repercussions if they engage in a sexual relationship with a current client.

I can't tell my dad I know West. I sure as hell can't confess to sleeping with the man in Las Vegas, not after what happened the last time I was there.

I push back from my chair and stand. "It's nice to meet you, Mr. Weston. As much as I hate admitting this in front of my father, I'm not opposed to day drinking."

My dad and Trent both let out a laugh.

West doesn't.

He doubles down. "We've met before."

I shake my head and lie through my teeth. "We haven't."

"I have the extra glass," Hal announces as he steps into the conference room. "You're all set."

West looks back at Hal before he turns toward me again. "I didn't get your name."

"Linny," I say quietly. "I'm Linny Faye."

West reaches out his hand. "I look forward to working with you, Linny."

I hesitate before I take his hand in mine, knowing that my body is going to react. My nipples are already hard and aching from the sound of his voice and the look in his eyes.

The moment I feel my hand brush his, wild desire races through me. I pull back and close my eyes to try and quiet the need to touch more of him.

"It's time to toast. Everyone grab a glass." Mitchell's voice cuts through the air.

I take a deep breath and open my eyes to find West smiling with two shot glasses in his hands. He offers one to me. I try to calm my shaking hand as I reach for it but it's futile.

He lifts his glass in the air, clinking it against mine. "To Vegas nights and New York days. Both are better with…"

"Rizon vanilla vodka," Trent interrupts.

I bring my glass to my lips and down the vodka in one swallow.

West watches intently, waiting until I place the glass down on the table before he leans closer and whispers, "Both are better with an angel."

My heart thuds as I look past him to where my dad, Mitchell, and Trent are gathered in a huddle pouring another round.

"I know it's you," West says smoothly. "You're a woman no man could ever forget."

CHAPTER FIFTEEN

JEREMY

SHE'S IGNORED me throughout this meeting.

The beautiful woman I fucked two months ago in Las Vegas is acting like she doesn't know me.

She's doing a piss poor job of it.

Her hair is a shade darker than it was the night we met and the eyeglasses she's wearing shield her gorgeous green eyes and long lashes, but I'd know her anywhere.

Everything about her is unforgettable. I have zero doubt in my mind that my Vegas angel is sitting across this conference table from me chewing on the end of a pen while Mitchell Bilton lays out some bullshit, lackluster plan to launch my vanilla vodka.

"I'm interested in hearing Linny's ideas," I interrupt Mitchell mid-sentence because I know what a goddamn television is and I'm not interested in paying hundreds of thousands of dollars to produce a thirty-second spot to air on a network channel during a game show that most of the population has never tuned into.

"I wasn't finished," Mitchell whines.

How old is this guy?

After two shots of vodka, his voice got higher and his words slurred together.

He's a lightweight and a selfish prick judging by the way he's monopolizing this meeting.

"I get the picture." I look in his direction. "You want to produce a commercial starring a couple of geriatric actors. Your suggestion is to not air it during football games. That's your plan, right?"

Mitchell nods and then shakes his head. "It might be better if we cast a couple of guys my age and showed it during games."

If I wanted to follow the same advertising path as Estey Vodka, I'd call his approach a win, but I'm looking for something fresh.

I lean forward and glance across the table at Linny. "What have you got for me?"

Her eyes meet mine, and I see a flicker of something; something that was there when I opened my hotel room door two months ago to find her.

My cock swells at the memory of how beautiful she was that night and how devastatingly sexy she is right now.

I want to clear the room and bend her over the table so I can finish what I started in Vegas. I need to touch her, taste her, fuck her.

"If your target demographic is my age, your primary focus should be on social media." Looking down, she brings the pen to her lips again.

I stare in fascination at the way her plump lips circle it

and the brief flashes of her pink tongue as she flicks it against the tip.

This is a first for me. I've never battled a hard-on in a meeting, but that's because I've never wanted a woman's mouth on my dick more.

"How old are you?" I blurt out.

She stiffens. "I'm within what should be your primary target market. Consumers between the ages of twenty-one and thirty-five are gravitating toward flavored vodkas. If your marketing efforts aren't appealing to them, you're wasting your time and your money."

"She's twenty-six."

I turn at the annoying sound of Mitchell's voice. I expected him to be passed out with his head on the table by now.

"My age isn't relevant." Linny's shoulders go back as she straightens in her chair. "I was referring to what I believe is Rizon's target consumer."

"Age is relevant." Mitchell's lips curl into a sneer. "With it comes experience and that's a requirement to handle an account this important."

Ignoring his comments, Linny faces me directly. "I've had a look at Rizon's social media accounts, and I see room for improvement, Mr. Weston. I'd strongly suggest you invest a good portion of your marketing budget in online ads. The people who will purchase your vanilla vodka use social media on a daily basis. You need to go where they are and create a buzz so they'll feel compelled to try the product."

She speaks the truth.

I've followed my grandfather's rulebook for too long.

He launched the company in an era where a billboard or magazine ad could sell hundreds of thousands of bottles of vodka.

I've piggybacked off his success, but our new products demand an innovative approach.

The time and attention we've devoted to social media have been extensive, but it's not enough. We need to do more.

"Also, I suggest we run a contest," she goes on, her gaze shifting to the bottle of vodka in the middle of the table. "It would be an easy way to engage our target market."

Our target market.

I know it's a job to her, but working side-by-side with her for this launch is exactly what I want.

"What will the prize be?" Mitchell asks.

The urge to knock the smirk off his face with my fist is strong. It's a wonder Faye & Sons has the reputation they do with this asshole as part of their team.

Linny waits a beat before she answers. "I have two ideas that I'd be more than happy to expand on with Trent."

"With Trent?" I sit back in my chair. If she thinks she's going to bypass me to work on the campaign with Trent, she's mistaken. I give her credit for maintaining her composure for the past hour, but she won't be able to keep it together once the hard work starts.

I'll get her to admit she's the woman I fucked before the ink is dry on my contract with Faye & Sons.

She looks at Trent. "I saw the contest you ran on your Instagram account when you were in Rio de Janeiro last fall. I suggest doing something similar on the official Rizon Vodka account. A bigger prize, and targeted advertising for a wider reach."

Rio de Janeiro? What the hell is she talking about?

Trent's expression says it all. Guilt mixed with embarrassment and something that borders on amusement.

I'm not about to call him out in this meeting, but the

smug son-of-a-bitch won't make it out of this building without confessing what he did in Rio.

"I like the way you think." He shoots Linny a smile. "Drop those ideas in an email and Jeremy and I will go over them."

"All we need is your signature on the dotted line, Mr. Weston," David chimes in. "I'll have my assistant bring in the contract and we can get started on the campaign first thing tomorrow morning."

"Linny leads this." I stand and button my suit jacket. "I'll work with the rest of your team, but she's our main point of contact."

I feel her gaze on me. I don't turn to look at her because my cock has finally dropped to half-mast. I want out of here so I can breathe and think.

"You've got yourself a deal." David rounds the table. "You're not going to be disappointed. Our firm will do whatever it takes to make Rizon vanilla vodka a success."

"Send the contract to my office." I motion for Trent to stand. "We're heading back there now."

"I'll hand deliver it." Mitchell pushes back from the table but stays seated. "Linny and I are a team. I'll be available whenever you need me day or night."

The only person in this room I want available day and night is silent. I turn toward her. She glides to her feet.

"It's been a pleasure to meet you, Mr. Weston." Her hand skims the waistband of her skirt. "I look forward to working with you, sir."

I look forward to fucking you. *Again.*

I bite back the urge to say that. "I'll be in touch."

She nods, parts her lips and lets out a soft breath.

I have no fucking idea how I'm going to keep it together

around her, but before the week is over, Linny Faye is going to confirm what I already know.

She's the woman I took to bed in Vegas and she's as eager to finish what we started as I am.

CHAPTER SIXTEEN

LINNY

"I KNOW I'm not who you were expecting, but I hope I'll do."

I smile at Jax Walker.

I left my office as soon as the meeting with West and Trent was over. I promised Ivy that I'd drop by her store, Whispers of Grace, to discuss the fall promotional campaign that we're set to launch next month.

"Ivy isn't here?" I ask the obvious question.

"Can I tell you a secret?" He leans in closer to me even though the only other person in the store is the assistant manager. She's in the stock room picking out new items for the bracelet display case.

"I'm an amazing secret keeper," I say honestly, holding up my right hand as if I'm taking a vow.

"My birthday is next month and my beautiful wife is planning a surprise party." His lips lift in a grin. "Right now she's at the bakery down the street ordering the cake. When she gets back, she'll tell you that she was at the café around the corner grabbing iced coffees for all of us."

I laugh lightly. "How do you know she's planning a surprise party?"

"Ivy is many things, but discreet isn't one of them." He chuckles. "I overheard her talking to my brother on the phone about it."

I've envied his relationship with his wife since I met them. He's her biggest supporter. Even though she runs the jewelry design business, he's always nearby if she needs guidance or another opinion.

He defers to her when it comes to every decision about this store and the others that she's opened. Jewelry may be Ivy's passion, but the man standing in front of me is her everything.

"I'm expecting you to act surprised when you're invited." He arches a dark brow. "Don't let me down, Linny."

"I'm not sure…I don't know if…" I fumble with what to say.

We have an amazing working relationship, but I can't tell if Ivy considers me more than a business contact or an acquaintance.

She's several years older than me and our shared interest is the ongoing success of her jewelry business.

I may have had dinner at their apartment yesterday, but that doesn't mean that she counts me as a friend.

"You're not sure if your name is on the guest list?" He finishes my question for me.

I nod.

"You remind Ivy a lot of herself." He brushes a piece of lint from the front of his navy blue suit jacket. "You're driven and determined. You won't take no for an answer and you haven't let this city change who you are."

I can't say that all of that is true, but I am committed to taking over for my father once he retires. Ivy knows that and she's been encouraging me to stay on course and keep my focus on my end goal.

"I admire her," I admit on a sigh. "She's one of the most successful women I've ever met."

"She knew what she wanted and she kept after it until it was in her grasp." He drags his left hand through his dark brown hair. My gaze catches on the simple band on his ring finger. "I'm grateful every day that she wanted me."

I look up and into his face. "The two of you are relationship goals."

"Relationship goals?"

I tilt my head to the side. "It's inspiring to see you together. I don't know anyone who wouldn't want a love like you share."

He nods slowly. "I'm a lucky man. I'm happier than I deserve to be."

I flash a smile. "The rest of us can only hope that one day we'll be as happy."

"I'll let you in on another secret." He narrows his gaze. "Technically, it's more of a heads-up."

"A heads-up?" I inhale deeply, trying to calm my nerves. I've been trembling since I left my office. Seeing West today shook my entire world. Staying focused on work is the only way I know how to cope.

If I think about the way he was looking at me in the conference room, I'll come undone and reach out to him. I can't do that. There's no way in hell Mitchell can ever find out that I know West on a very personal level.

My dad will have no choice but to pull me off the Rizon Vodka campaign and hand it over to my stepbrother.

I need that account to help prove that I'm a better pick for CEO than Mitchell will ever be.

Jax nods. "Ivy's been dying to set you up with a friend of ours."

I should be used to it by now. Harmony isn't the only woman in my life who has taken it upon herself to find my soul mate. My sister, Bethy, has done the same thing for years. Living halfway across the world in Australia hasn't stopped her. She still texts me pictures of single men that her friends in Manhattan know in the hope that I'll agree to meet one.

I haven't yet.

"I'm kind of seeing someone," I say because I don't want to mix business with pleasure.

If I agree to meet up with their friend and we don't hit it off, I'll run the risk of offending Ivy, Jax or both of them.

It's not worth it.

"What's his name?"

West. A part of me is tempted to say that just so I can hear his name coming from my lips again.

"Roland." I opt for the safe choice since I'll be seeing him again in a few days and it's not a total lie.

"The four of us should do dinner." He glances over his shoulder at the door to the store. "As soon as Ivy gets back, we'll set something up."

Dammit.

I think I just arranged my third date with Roland Elgar, even though the man I can't stop thinking about is Jeremy Weston.

CHAPTER SEVENTEEN

JEREMY

I HAVEN'T BEEN able to get Linny Faye out of my mind.

After I got back to my office earlier, I did what any rational man with a raging erection would do.

I locked my private bathroom door and pumped one out to the vision of Linny on the bed in my hotel room.

I'll never forget the way that woman looks nude.

I'm grateful for that since it's been my sole source of masturbation inspiration since I got back from Las Vegas.

After I cleaned up, I tore into Trent about the unauthorized contest he held when he was in Rio de Janeiro last year.

He posted a selfie on Instagram offering a free drink and a year's supply of our traditional vodka to whoever met him at a local bar first.

According to him, the bar was overrun with customers. They pulled in more money that night than they had in years. To repay Trent, they offered to carry our vodka exclusively in all of their locations in Brazil.

I wondered how he landed that deal.

The free case of vodka sent to an address in Rio makes a lot more sense now too.

"Why are you still here?" Blythe pokes her heard into my office. "It's late. Go home."

I look down at my watch. "I'm the boss. I can stay as late as I want. You know I don't pay overtime so why the hell aren't you home with Harve?"

She shrugs as she settles into one of the chairs opposite my desk. "It's poker night."

"Harve plays?" I lean back. "I play with Rocco and a few of his friends twice a month."

She claps her hands together once. "You do? Are spectators allowed?"

"Not if they're dressed like that. You look like a candy cane, Blythe."

No exaggeration.

She's wearing a white dress with red diagonal stripes topped off with a green scarf around her neck.

As usual, she ignores my critique of her wardrobe without batting an eyelash. "Harve could use some new poker buddies. He's always beating the three he plays with now."

"He's good?"

"The best," she answers proudly. "He has yet to meet anyone who can out -bluff him."

I point out the obvious. "Rocco is a former world poker champion. Harve wouldn't stand a chance against him."

"I bet he would." Her eyebrows dance.

She'll lose that bet. The same way that I almost always lose when I play cards with Rocco. I tell myself I'm doing it for fun and as a way to unwind, but every single time I leave his place with an empty wallet, I wonder where the hell I left my better judgment.

"Invite Harve to your next game and we can set up a side wager," she goes on. "If he wins, you give me an extra week off this year with pay."

Curiosity drives the next words out of my mouth. "And if Harve loses?"

"I'll bring you coffee every morning for a month."

I can't help but laugh. "That's in your goddamn job description."

"Is it?"

I glance down at my watch again. "Text Conrad to pick you up. It's time to call it a day."

"I can charge it to Rizon?" She skims her thumb over the screen of her smartphone.

I nod. "Tell your grandson to take you to Crispy Biscuit. It's a diner in midtown. Buy him a grilled cheese and fries. Order yourself some dinner too."

"You're buying?" She looks up from her phone. "Why are you in such a good mood?"

I found my Vegas angel today.

I skip over honesty and settle on believable. "I locked down one of the best advertising firms in the city to handle the vanilla vodka campaign."

"That is good news." She places her phone back in her lap. "Con is five minutes away. I'll grab my things and head down to the lobby."

I stand. "I'll see you tomorrow morning."

She's on her feet too. "Don't stay too late, Jeremy."

I won't take her advice. I'll order something in and focus on the budget projections for next quarter. "I'll see to it Harve has a seat at our next poker game."

"I'm tagging along," she says as she turns to leave my office. "I want to see the look on Rocco's face when Harve wins."

I want to see that look too, but I doubt it'll happen.

"Enjoy your night, Blythe."

She turns back to face me. "She must be special."

I lift my chin. "Who?"

"The woman you keep thinking about." She shoots me a warm look. "I've been around the block enough times to know when a man's mind is caught up with a beautiful woman."

I should deny it, but I don't. "She's very beautiful."

"Why don't you take your own advice and get out of here? Meet her for dinner."

Because she won't even admit that I know her.

I could confess all of this to Blythe, but I've always kept my personal life out of the office. That won't change now.

"Don't keep Con waiting. I'm footing the bill, remember?"

She laughs. "You're politely trying to tell me to mind my own business."

"Since when am I polite?" I lean against the edge of my desk.

"Good point." She tugs on the ends of her scarf. "I'll see you tomorrow?"

"Bright and early, Blythe."

CHAPTER EIGHTEEN

LINNY

I REREAD the cryptic text message that my dad sent me an hour ago.

Dad: Be at Calvetti's at noon. Urgent.

I didn't notice the message until ten minutes ago since I spent the morning at Whispers of Grace with Ivy working on the upcoming promo campaign.

We were supposed to do that last night, but when she came back to her store empty-handed and in a panic about her daughter, Jacey, having a fever, she rushed back out with Jax on her heel.

I checked in with them before I went to bed and everything was fine. Jacey was fast asleep and fever free.

That's when Ivy asked if I could swing by the store first thing this morning to finalize which images to use for the promo.

I showed up with two coffees in hand and a box of pastries.

After setting the ringer on my phone to silent, we got to work. We settled on a handful of photographs that I'll send to our graphic designer so she can work her magic and create a series of online ads.

I'm ordering a revamp of the Whispers of Grace website too since I landed Ivy a spot on a national morning show where she'll show off her newest designs.

As I exit the subway, I glance down at my phone's screen again.

There's nothing.

My dad hasn't responded to my text. I asked him why he arranged the sudden lunch date at his favorite Italian restaurant.

The last time this happened, he asked me to meet him so he could tell me that he was planning on proposing to Diane.

He wanted my blessing. I tearfully gave it to him without question, thrilled that he'd found love again.

My parents divorced when I was ten years old, but they made the transition as easy as they could for my sister and me. If they ever argued it wasn't within earshot of Bethy or me.

They wanted the best for each other. My dad found that in Diane. My mom is still searching. Her quest landed her in Bora Bora six months ago and in the arms of a man a decade younger than her who is teaching her everything he knows about scuba diving and love.

She's happy. I can't ask for more than that.

I round the corner and spot the familiar red and white checkered awning of Calvetti's halfway down the block.

I'm not dressed for racing around Manhattan.

I put on a simple black sheath dress this morning and paired that with red stilettos. Since I only got twenty minutes of sleep last night, I didn't attempt to shove my contact lenses into my bloodshot eyes.

I'm wearing the same eyeglasses I was yesterday and my hair is loose and wavy. I should have grabbed the blow dryer and straightener after my shower this morning, but I spent too much time online researching everything I could find out about Jeremy Weston.

I didn't make it past the images.

Thinking about him kept me up most of the night, and seeing dozens of pictures of him at different galas and benefits made me ache to be back in that hotel room with him.

Jeremy Weston in a tuxedo is better than I imagined.

I yank open the door to Calvetti's and freeze.

Jeremy Weston in a dark blue suit with a white dress shirt and light blue tie isn't half bad either.

Now I know exactly why my dad wanted me to meet him here. He's sitting at a table with West and Trent.

The second West spots me he's on his feet and approaching me from across the restaurant. As he nears where I'm standing, a smile touches his full lips.

Why does he have to be so handsome?

"Angel," he whispers roughly. "You look beautiful today."

My heart pounds fiercely in my chest. I can't do this. I can't give in to the temptation to acknowledge what we both already know. We fucked two months ago and I've spent hours since then thinking about every detail of that night.

"It's nice to see you again, Mr. Weston." My voice is strained.

The corner of his mouth lifts into a smile. "What happened in Vegas isn't going to stay there."

"Vegas?" I squeak the word out.

"Vegas? What about Las Vegas?"

We both turn at the sound of Mitchell's voice. He's standing in the entrance of the restaurant with his hand still curled around the doorknob.

"What are you two talking about?" He moves closer, the door shutting behind him. "Tell me what I'm missing here."

I close my eyes because the relentless hammering of my heart inside my chest is deafening. I need to get a grip.

"One of the ideas I've been batting around with Trent is a launch party on the strip."

My eyes pop open at West's words.

"That's brilliant." Mitchell moves to stand next to me. "Why didn't I think of that? It's the perfect way to launch the vanilla vodka."

It's also the perfect way to launch any new tequila brand, or bourbon, or beer, which is why it's the go-to marketing move for so many companies.

It works, but it's not for Rizon.

"I think we should have a launch party here in Manhattan. There's a beautiful rooftop terrace on the Bishop Hotel in Tribeca. We could do it at dusk, and make it a black tie affair."

I'm mildly impressed with myself for coming up with that in a split second.

Mitchell shakes his head. "I don't like it. My vote is for Vegas."

West turns his attention back to me, his gaze scanning my face. "My vote is for Manhattan. I don't need to get on an airplane to get what I want."

His words hold more meaning than Mitchell can comprehend. Maybe more than I can.

West wants me.

His desire is there in his eyes and woven into everything he says to me.

He has no idea that I'm trying to win the fight of my life against Mitchell, and I can't risk losing that, not even for him.

CHAPTER NINETEEN

JEREMY

BY SOME WELCOME twist of fate, I'm sitting next to Linny for lunch. The circular table was set for four, but Mitchell invited himself along once he got word from David's assistant that a working lunch was going down at Calvetti's.

I didn't want him here.

I made that clear to David when I spoke to him this morning. This lunch was his idea, as was the restaurant choice.

After agreeing to meet at Calvetti's at noon, I told David that I wanted Linny here, but I didn't see any need to include Mitchell.

This is designed to be a casual meeting so we can discuss the broad scope of the upcoming campaign.

In other words, it's a repeat of yesterday but with pasta.

Good pasta.

Judging by the look of pure satisfaction on Linny's face, she thinks it's great pasta.

Mitchell elbows me again which sends a drop of tomato

sauce in motion. It flies from the rigatoni noodle on my fork onto my pristine tie; my three hundred dollar pristine light blue tie.

"Shit," I mutter under my breath as I reach to dab the spot with my napkin.

"No." Linny shakes her head. "Don't do that. You're making it worse."

How the hell can it get any worse?

My tie is ruined, they don't serve Rizon vodka here, and my dick is painfully hard since the side of Linny's thigh has been brushing against mine for the last thirty minutes.

Add to that the fact that Mitchell has monopolized the conversation with stories about his time working at an Italian restaurant in Brooklyn when he was in high school.

The guy is looking for a gold medal because he can toss pizza dough.

"We'll cover the cost of having it dry cleaned," Linny offers. "If you take it off, I'll have it cleaned and back to your office by the end of the day."

I look over at her, after quickly glancing at Mitchell who is muttering something under his breath. "You'll bring it to my office by the end of the day?"

She shakes her head. "They can deliver."

"Of course Linny will bring it to you," David says, pointing at his daughter. "I'm responsible since pasta for lunch was my idea. Calvetti's should have a warning on the menu about the collateral damage that can result from enjoying an order of baked rigatoni."

I unknot my tie and slip it from around my neck. "I appreciate you doing this, Linny."

She takes the tie when I slide it into her hands. "Of course, Mr. Weston. It's the least we can do."

She avoids eye contact, so I turn, but not before I catch a

quick glimpse of her subtly raising the tie to her face before she closes her eyes and inhales the scent.

Everyone else at the table would mistake it for her taking a closer look at the stain. I take it for what it is and that's a reminder of my cologne.

It's the same cologne I was wearing the night we fucked.

————

NINETY MINUTES later I glance down at my watch. "I'm going to need the name of your dry cleaner. He or she is a fucking wizard."

"A wizard?" Linny looks at the black box in my hand.

"We left Calvetti's an hour ago and you just brought me this." I tip my chin toward the light blue silk tie that's folded with care in the box.

"Oh." Her mouth forms a perfect O-shape.

I want to slide my dick right in, past those plump lips and over her pink tongue until she takes it all.

"The tie couldn't be saved." She sighs nervously. "I purchased a new one for you."

Impressive, but not necessary.

I have too many ties to count. The loss of one isn't worth the effort it took her to replace it, but then again, it is worth this.

Linny Faye, my Vegas angel, is standing in my office.

"Thank you," I offer because I am a grateful son-of-a-bitch when it's warranted.

"You're welcome." She shoulders her black purse. "I need to get back to my office."

"Angel?"

Her head pops up. "My name is Linny, Mr. Weston."

I brush past her to close my office door. I don't want to

broadcast this conversation. I trust Blythe to keep her mouth shut if she overhears something she shouldn't. I don't trust anyone else who works on this floor to do the same.

"I have to go." Linny turns to face me. "I have a meeting in thirty minutes."

"It's just the two of us." I wave my hand in a circle in the space between us. "Cut the bullshit. I know it's you. You know it's you, so why the act?"

Her bottom lip quivers in a way that makes me want to sink my teeth into it. "I don't know what you're talking about."

I inch closer to her. "You know exactly what I'm talking about. You in a tutu and tiara, me in my birthday suit. Us in my bed in Vegas."

Her eyes widen with shock. She does the song and dance a second time, this time with a shake in her voice. "I said that I don't know what you're talking about."

"Even superheroes can't hide who they really are behind a pair of eyeglasses." I lean closer. "I would know you anywhere, angel."

She reaches up to touch the frame of her glasses. "You have me mixed up with someone else."

"Do you have a sister?"

She nods. "Bethy."

"Is she your twin?"

"No. She's two years older than me." Her tongue glosses over her lips.

Jesus. I want a taste of that.

"She's not nearly as beautiful as you, is she?" My eyes are locked to hers.

She crosses her arms. "Bethy is beautiful."

"But not as beautiful as you," I stress the last word.

"I wouldn't say that." Her gaze drops to the floor.

"I would." I push because I want to know why. I want to know why in the hell she won't admit that we fucked.

She lets out a breathy sigh. "You don't even know what she looks like."

"It doesn't matter what she looks like."

Her brows shoot up. "What do you mean it doesn't matter what she looks like?"

"She can't be more beautiful than you." I lean so close that my breath whispers over her cheek. "There isn't a woman on this earth who is more beautiful than you."

She doesn't say a word, but her eyes give something away. A brief flicker of the want I saw in Vegas is there before it disappears with a shake of her head.

"You can pretend all you want." I inch back and look her over. "My body will never forget you."

Her hand jumps to her chest. "I need to go."

I study her, frustration gnawing at me. I could push her more, but she's not ready to admit we spent the night together. She has her reasons. I have patience, although in a limited quantity.

"Thank you again for the tie, Linny."

"Of course." Her eyes skim the box in my hands. "I'm sorry that Mitchell messed up the other one."

"I'm not." I toss the tie box onto my desk. "It brought you here. It gave us a chance to talk privately."

Not that it did any good. It's obvious that when Linny Faye lies, she commits to it body and soul.

She approaches my office door, so I ask the question I'm not sure I want to know the answer to. "Have you ever done something you regret?"

She stops and it takes a beat before she turns to face me. "We all have regrets, don't we?"

"I spent a night in Vegas with an incredible woman two

months ago." I stroke my jaw. "I regret falling asleep before I could get her name and number because I've thought about her every day since."

She swallows hard, her gaze meeting mine, but before a word can leave her lips, Blythe barges in and the moment is lost.

"Mr. Weston, I hate to interrupt, but there's a situation that needs your attention." Blythe's gaze volleys between Linny and me.

"It can wait," I bark back.

"I have to go." Linny brushes past Blythe on her way out of my office before she rounds the corner and disappears from sight.

"What the hell, Blythe?" I rake both hands through my hair in aggravation. "You know how I feel about knocking before you come in."

"You have a call, Jeremy." She points at my desk phone. "It's Athena. She said it's urgent."

"Leave." I wave my hand in the air. "Out."

She scurries away and closes the door behind her as I drop into my chair and bring the phone to my ear.

CHAPTER TWENTY

Linny

IT'S BEEN three hours since I left West's office, and I'm still feeling drunk on his words.

It took every ounce of willpower in my body not to grab him by the lapels of his suit jacket, tug him closer and kiss him.

God, did I want to kiss that man.

I couldn't stop thinking about him as I sat through a meeting with a legacy client who refuses to talk to anyone but me.

She was one of the first clients of Faye & Sons back when my grandfather ran the company.

He chose the name in the hope that his two then high-school aged sons would follow in his footsteps. My dad did. My uncle, Tom, became a nuclear physicist. From what I've heard from my dad, my granddad didn't complain about Tom's career choice once.

"How was your meeting with Mary?" My dad strolls into my office with a grin on his face.

If I were a fan of poodles and quilting, I'd call it a success.

Mary has been retired for years. The fabric store chain she founded is the largest in the country and the team that is running it, is one of the best.

I touch base with the head of their internal marketing team twice a year to offer help if they need it. They occasionally do, but I'll never turn down a meeting with Mary.

She was instrumental in helping my late granddad find the success he did.

"It's always nice to visit with her." I push up from my chair. "You look especially happy this afternoon."

"I think Diane and I found the perfect place on the Gulf Coast."

My stomach knots, but I keep a smile on my face.

Seeing my dad this excited warms my heart, but there's a part of me that wants him to stay in Manhattan. Some of that longing stems from the struggle over control of the company once he's gone, but it's more than that.

My dad has always been the steady hand that guides me. He's been there if I need someone to talk to in a coffee shop at midnight or Central Park in the middle of a Sunday afternoon.

I rely on him and when he's no longer a taxi ride away, I know I'll miss him.

"What's it like?" I ask because I want to keep the ear-to-ear grin on his face.

He tugs his smartphone out of the pocket of his brown suit jacket. "Diane sent me the real estate listing. I want your honest opinion."

I stare at him before my gaze drops to his phone. I skim my finger over the screen, scrolling through image after image of a gorgeous beach house with wide-open ocean views.

This is my dad's dream. It's always been his dream.

"I think you found your forever home, dad," I whisper.

He slides the phone back into his palm. "I can't say that Florida and I will agree on everything, but this is a place where I can see the blue sky and hear the ocean."

I study his face. He's just as handsome as he was when I was a little girl.

"I'm happy for you." I rub my chest to chase away the ache I feel when I think about him living so far away from me. "I'm happy for both of you."

"Diane wants you to help her with the interior design." His brows wiggle. "She's always saying that you have the best eye."

Diane is a gracious woman who works extra hard to include Bethy and me in my dad's life. She's always gone out of her way to make sure we know that we're an essential part of her life too.

"I'll help in any way I can." I glance down at my dad's phone when it chimes.

His gaze follows mine. "It's Jeremy Weston."

I tilt my head to try and get a better look at what the message says, but my dad brings the phone so close to his face, that whatever is on the screen is obstructed from my view.

He refuses to wear reading glasses.

"He wanted to thank us again for how we handled the tie situation at lunch." He squints as his eyes skim the phone's screen, confusion knitting his brow. "You replaced the tie? He wrote that you bought him a brand new tie."

"It was the right thing to do." I smile softly. "Getting tomato sauce out of silk is almost impossible."

"So you tossed the stained tie?" He lowers his phone.

Into my purse so I can smell West's cologne whenever I want.

"I took care of it." I wait a beat, and then continue, "I spoke to Jeremy earlier about having the vanilla vodka launch party at the Bishop Hotel in Tribeca. I thought a black-tie affair on their rooftop terrace at dusk would be ideal."

My dad's eyes widen. "Classy and elegant. What was Jeremy's take on it?"

I look down at the floor. Every time I hear my dad say his name it's jarring. He has no idea that I had a one-night stand with West or that I was even in Las Vegas that weekend. He was in Paris with Diane for a two-week anniversary celebration when I jetted off to Sin City.

"He seemed receptive," I answer with a sigh. "I'll put together a more extensive description of the event and possible guest list and we can revisit it the next time we meet with him."

He glances at his phone again when it chimes. "Don't you mean the next time you meet him, sweetheart? That's tomorrow night, right?

I arch both brows. "Tomorrow night?"

He spins his phone's screen around so it's facing me. I lean in and read the text message. Twice.

Jeremy Weston: *Linny and I are having dinner tomorrow. I do my best work one-on-one, and Linny understands exactly what I want.*

Jerk.

"I don't have to tell you how impressed I am by the initiative you're showing on this account." My dad beams as he slips the phone back into his pocket. "You're making me proud and your granddad would say the same if he were here."

My granddad would be horrified if he knew why West was intent on arranging dinner for the two of us behind my back.

"You'll fill me in on everything you discuss with Jeremy, won't you?"

I stare at my dad. I can't answer that truthfully so I edge around it. "I'll put together a condensed version of our conversation about the launch party and have it on your desk first thing Friday morning."

"Remember to order a glass of Rizon at the restaurant." He winks. "Impressing the client is always the end game."

I'd normally agree with him, but in this case, beating the client at his own game is a temptation I may not be able to resist.

"I've got this, dad," I say with no conviction at all.

"I know you do." He gives me a curt nod. "You always make me proud."

CHAPTER TWENTY-ONE

Linny

JEREMY WESTON STOOD ME UP.

Dammit. He stood me up after I went to all the trouble of arranging a mini preview party of the vanilla vodka launch.

I called my contact in guest relations at the Bishop Hotel Tribeca and asked if I could rent the terrace for two hours tonight. She agreed without question, even offering the space for free. I was hoping she would after all the extra work I did for them during the launch of their new hotel on the Lower East Side earlier this year.

After I blasted out a text invitation to eight of my contacts in the food industry in Manhattan, I set up a private tasting bar for Rizon vanilla vodka.

The evening was complete with two servers, a decadent platter of caviar, and soft music.

It was an intimate prelude to the main event. That will take place in a few weeks, on the eve of the vodka's official launch.

Everyone at the party was a potential new contact for Jeremy.

It was a foolproof idea since Jeremy had reached out to me via text late yesterday afternoon telling me that he wanted to meet for dinner at Axel Tribeca at seven p.m. tonight.

The restaurant is in the same hotel I'm planning on having the launch party, so it seemed like a great way to showcase my idea to him and avoid another round of twenty questions about why I won't admit I'm the woman he slept with in Vegas.

I texted him back and said I would see him tonight.

His reply was instant. He was looking forward to having dinner with me.

That was the last I heard from him.

It was Trent who showed up in the lobby of the hotel looking for me with a weak excuse about a situation that only his boss could handle.

He offered Jeremy's sincerest apologies before he spent the next two hours telling me how impressed he was by my trial run of the launch party.

I didn't do it for him.

I did it to show West that our relationship is strictly business.

It's exhausting pretending I'm not the woman he slept with in Vegas. I don't know how much longer I can do it, but when I do finally confess, I want there to be an immediate understanding between us.

He needs to be on the same page as me and that's one where we don't fuck again.

I can't risk my future over great sex.

I watch as the last guest boards the elevator that will take them back down to the lobby.

"I wish Jeremy could have seen this." Trent waves his

arm in the air. "The bright lights of the city, the cool breeze, our vodka flowing freely. The launch party is going to be one for the record books."

I skim my palm over the front of the black lace dress I'm wearing. I took more time than I should have getting ready for tonight. Logically, I know that West and I can't pick up where we left off in Vegas, but I don't mind the way he looks at me.

"I took some pictures. I'll forward them to you so you can show them to Jeremy when you see him."

"I'm on my way to see him now." Trent takes one last sip from his glass, swallowing the vodka that was left. "He's going to love this, Linny. Seriously, you did a great job."

I want to ask if the situation West was dealing with is resolved, but I bite my tongue. I don't want to admit to myself that I'm disappointed that he didn't show up. It stings even more than it should because West was under the impression that he was meeting me for a quiet dinner.

This is exactly what I wanted, so why is it bothering me?

"Thank you," I reply with a smile. "I'm glad you could make it tonight."

"Me too." He places the glass down on a table. "I'm going to head out, but I'll reach out to you early next week to hammer down the details for the launch. I want everything in place before we round the homestretch."

I nod in silence.

Tonight was a big win for my career, so why do I feel like I've lost something?

———

"THIS WAS JUST DELIVERED for you, Linny."

My head pops up at the sound of Hal's voice. He's

standing in the open doorway of my office with a broad grin on his face and a square white box in his hands.

"Loretta wasn't at her desk." He glances over his shoulder at my assistant's empty chair. "I signed for it."

I push back from my desk and stand. "Thanks for doing that, Hal. How's your day going?"

I only ask because the poor man is on a tight leash held by Mitchell. Hal is brilliant in his own right, but Mitchell has kept him tied to the position of his executive assistant for years.

Hal would never admit it, but I'm convinced that many of the commendable ideas that Mitchell has come up with were born in Hal's imagination.

"You know," he says with an exaggerated laugh. "It's Friday, so there's that."

I straighten the skirt of my navy blue dress. "Do you have big weekend plans?"

"Mitchell's never asked me that," he says quietly, pushing the box at me. "I'm going to a film festival in Brooklyn."

"Sounds fun." I glance at the box. There's nothing on the outside that identifies who sent it. "Did this arrive in an envelope?"

"No." He shakes his head. "The delivery guy said he needed a signature from you or your assistant. That's all I know."

Anxiety pricks at me. I'd classify this as a surprise, and as usual, I'm not thrilled by the prospect of that. "Thanks again, Hal."

I wait for him to take the hint and leave. He does.

"Have a good weekend, Linny."

"You too," I say under my breath as he walks back through the doorway.

I rush to shut the door, not wanting anyone else to stroll into my office unexpectedly.

I set the box on my desk and stare at it. Clients have sent me thank you gifts in the past, but this feels different.

Pulling on the corner of the silver ribbon, I feel my heart beat quicken. I lift the top of the box off to find a pillow of pink tissue paper.

I pause for a second before I grab two of the ends and separate the paper.

Something glimmers when the overhead light in my office hits it, just as the realization of what it is, hits me.

It's the tiara.

The plastic, cheap tiara that I had on my head in Las Vegas, and left in West's hotel suite is now sitting on my desk.

My hands shake as I reach for the small white envelope tucked next to the tiara. Sliding out the card, I take a deep breath.

The handwriting is bold and masculine, the message concise and to the point.

You in this tiara: beautiful.
You in my bed in Vegas: breathtaking.

I close my eyes to try and stop the flood of memories of that night. I want it again. I want him again, but that can't happen.

I throw the card back into the box, slide the lid on and put it all in the bottom drawer of my desk.

What happened in Vegas with West is in my past. That's where it needs to stay.

CHAPTER TWENTY-TWO

JEREMY

THE PACKAGE I sent to Linny should have arrived at her office by now. I called the delivery service myself and gave the guy specific instructions.

I wanted the box in Linny's hands, not in anyone else's, but even the best-laid plan can fall off the rails. I knew there was a slim chance that someone else could inadvertently or deliberately open it.

I didn't sign my name on the card for that reason.

Putting her in a compromising position at work isn't my intention. It took me a few minutes during our initial meeting in the conference room to realize that she didn't want her dad knowing about our past connection.

She was stoic and determined that day, but since then I've seen small flashes of the woman I fucked in Las Vegas.

I was hoping that last night over dinner, she'd finally confess and tell me why in the hell she's acting like our one-night stand never happened.

The sole reason can't be because she's trying to shield her wild side from her father. If that were the case, she would have dropped the act when we were alone. There's more to this.

It's not that I'm craving the ego boost that comes with a woman remembering how great I am in bed.

I'm not looking for that with her.

I want an acknowledgment of what happened between us two months ago so we can have an honest discussion about how to handle our working relationship. Once that's been established, I want more nights like the one we had in Vegas. I'd bet everything I own, that she does too.

"I'm back," Trent announces as he enters my office. "Sorry for running out earlier. Duty called."

We sat down an hour ago to go over what happened last night when he went to Axel Tribeca to meet Linny for dinner.

I sent him in my place because canceling altogether wasn't an option after I realized I had to bail and after hearing about all the trouble Linny had gone to.

Julian Bishop, the owner of the Bishop Hotel chain, called me late yesterday afternoon to congratulate me on the upcoming launch of the vanilla vodka.

He told me that he was happy to offer the terrace free of charge for the intimate tasting party Rizon was having last night.

Our grandfathers were friends, which carried over to the two of us. We're not close by any means, but when either of us asks a favor, the other is quick to help.

"As long as it's business related, I have no problem with it or with the fact that you're texting during this meeting," I say as I point at his phone. "You're texting, not gaming, right?"

He looks up, his fingers still tapping out a message on the

screen. "I'm locking down an app. It'll be released the same day as the vanilla vodka launch."

"An app? What app?"

"The Rizon app. It's going to be primarily user driven. Our customers will be able to pinpoint locations our products are served, upload their vodka cocktail recipes and pictures. That's basic surface stuff. There's a lot more to it." He drops the phone into his pocket. "It was Linny's idea. She mentioned it last night."

"Really?"

"Really." He takes a seat. "I reached out to a developer today. I told him I need a rush on it. He said he'd do it for the right price."

The impulse is there to shut this down before it goes any further, but it's a viable idea that will broaden our reach. Being outside the loop isn't a place I'm familiar with, but I'll defer to Trent on this, only because he's invested enough in it that I know he'll see it through.

"You trust the guy you're hiring?" I scratch my brow.

He rubs his palm over his thigh. "He's already signed all the standard forms. He'll keep quiet, get the job done and cash his check."

"Jot down all the app ideas in an email before you leave for the day and send it to me."

"Will do." He exhales. "I'm glad everything worked out last night."

He knows better than to delve into my personal life. He wanted to meet at a coffee shop around the corner from my apartment after he was done at the impromptu tasting party. I turned him down.

He attempts to play the concerned friend, but that's not who he is to me. He's an employee who happened to overhear me talking to my attorney about my father once.

Since then, I've kept him close and paid him well, because I trust that he'll keep quiet if his bank account is healthy.

He tugs his phone out of his pocket again. "I'll send you the pictures I took at the Bishop Tribeca last night. There's a couple in there that Linny took of the bar setup. We'll need to work on lighting and bring in some greenery, but overall I think it's got the look and feel we want for the launch party."

I don't react when I hear a string of chimes from my phone signaling the images he's sending have arrived.

"Don't forget to put that email together before you take off, Trent."

He nods, his gaze still glued to his phone. "Will do. I'll see you on Monday?"

"If you make it through the weekend." I laugh as he pushes to his feet. "I heard you're headed out of town to see your brother."

He scrubs a hand over the back of his neck. "My brother, his wife and their six kids. I hope to hell I live through the next two days."

Grabbing my phone, I scroll through the pictures he sent as he walks out of my office. I don't need a refresher on what the terrace at the Bishop Hotel looks like. I've been. Twice.

The first time it was for the wedding of a friend. The second time was a fundraising gala organized by one of the charities I support. I donated the vodka for the event and a sizable check.

I pause when I reach an image of Linny.

She's smiling as she stands next to Trent. From the camera's angle it's obvious he's the one who captured the shot.

His arm is wrapped around her shoulder. *Fuck him.*

Her hair is blowing in the wind.

She's not wearing eyeglasses.

I pinch my fingers against the screen to zoom in on her beautiful face.

This is what she looked like the night I opened the door of my hotel room in Las Vegas.

Carefree, wild, uninhibited, and breathtakingly gorgeous.

I could have been the one with her last night, calling her out on her bullshit.

I curse under my breath for missing my chance to meet her at Axel Tribeca, but I had no choice.

I'll find another opportunity to get Linny alone and when I do, she's not leaving the room until she admits that we spent the night together.

Then, I want a repeat.

CHAPTER TWENTY-THREE

LINNY

I RACE up the sidewalk toward Nova. I was supposed to meet Roland twenty minutes ago, but my Uber driver didn't show.

Instead of calling for another car, I hopped on the subway in my new red dress and matching heels.

It took longer than I expected to walk from the subway station to here, but I finally made it.

I peer inside the front window of the restaurant but I don't spot my date anywhere.

After I opened the box from West, debating whether or not to cancel on Roland ate up most of my afternoon

I couldn't get West out of my mind. That made me feel a rush of guilt over meeting another man, but this evening isn't just about getting to know Roland better.

It's a chance for me to enjoy some decadent food, drink good wine and relax after the brutal week I've had.

Taking on a new client is hard enough. When you had an

amazing one-night stand with them, it makes everything that much more complicated.

Everything.

"Linny, over here."

I turn at the sound of Roland's voice. I recognize it right away, even though nothing about it is extraordinary.

"Roland," I call out as I raise my hand in his direction.

I see him pushing his way through a crowd of people gathered on the sidewalk outside Nova.

As he approaches, I steel myself for our greeting. We haven't kissed yet. The only physical contact we've had was a handshake the night we met and the brief hug we shared when we said goodbye in this spot almost a week ago.

He looks nice, handsome.

He's dressed in dark jeans, a blue button-down shirt that's open at the collar and a black blazer.

Women turn to look at him as he nears me, but those butterflies that I know should be flipping around in my stomach, aren't there.

He goes in for a hug and I'm instantly grateful that it's not more.

"You look gorgeous." He pulls back and looks me over. "I have a surprise waiting for you inside."

I've had my quota of surprises for this year.

I smile and wiggle my brows. "Give me a little hint."

He taps the tip of my nose and I instantly know that any spark that might have caught fire between us has been extinguished. Forever.

The finger on the end of my nose is a classic move.

My dad has done it to me since I was a little girl.

He reaches for my hand and I let him take it while I run through the '*we should be friends*' speech in my head.

I'll need to give it before the end of the night, so it doesn't hurt to rehearse mentally.

We push our way through the line of people near the front door. I have no idea why Roland thinks he can leapfrog to the front, but I don't complain because I haven't eaten anything but a bagel all day.

I'm famished and thirsty. I need a burger and a glass of wine.

"Over there." Roland points as soon as we enter the restaurant. "Look over there, Linny."

I do.

My empty stomach sinks.

Jeremy Weston, looking as hot as ever in black pants and a gray lightweight V-neck sweater, is standing in my direct line of sight. Wrapped around his forearm are a woman's hands.

I can only see her profile, but that's enough. Tight black dress, sky-high heels, long blonde hair and curves for days.

I look over at Roland and shrug.

Is the man a mind reader? Did he figure out that I'm stuck on West and not him?

"I'm not sure what," I pause because the only thing I'm sure of is that I don't want to be here.

"Look again. She's coming this way," Roland says, his finger waving in the air again, right toward where West and the blonde are.

I look because I have nothing to lose at this point.

"Oh my god, Linny," Harmony screams as she races at me. "Surprise."

I grab hold of her when she takes me in her arms, grateful for the familiar face. I scan the area behind her for West, but he's gone.

It's probably for the best. He was with someone else.

Why did I think he would chase after me forever? I've spent every second we've been together pretending I'm not the woman he took to bed in Vegas.

I had one night with the man. That's all I'll ever have.

———

"IT LOOKS like you two are hitting it off." Harmony beams with pride, her gaze volleying between Roland and me. "You were holding hands when you walked in. How adorable is that?"

I shoot her a look, but she misses it because she's too caught up in congratulating herself for setting the two of us up.

"Linny is everything any guy could ever want." Roland wraps his arm around my shoulder. "She's beautiful, smart and she loves surprises."

Harmony giggles. "Linny loves surprises? Since when?"

"Since never." I sigh. I wish I could step out of Roland's reach, but I don't want to embarrass him.

He went out of his way to arrange this evening for me. I had no idea that Harmony was going to be at Nova tonight. When she texted me earlier to wish me a great second date with Roland, she didn't give anything away.

"Do you like my new dress?" She twirls in place.

It's pretty. Royal blue suits her. The fitted sheath dress matches the color of Rueben's tie perfectly. They went to a lot of trouble to get ready for this, so I need to brush off what I'm feeling about seeing West with another woman and get my head back in the moment.

"It's beautiful." I reach for her hand. "I'm really glad you're here."

"Let's get these ladies some wine." Roland pats Rueben on the back. "I'm sensing they need a little private girl time."

Rueben grunts and tosses Harmony a wink.

She leans into me, waiting until the men are out of earshot before she speaks. "Rueben is so getting lucky tonight. Is Roland?"

I narrow my eyes. "Not with me."

She laughs with such force that for a second I think it's fake, but it's not. I can tell because of the snort that escapes her.

"Harmony," I say her name, my tone firm and low. I should tell her right now that I'm not interested in Roland, but he deserves to hear that from me and not her. I need a few minutes to think without anyone around. There's only one place in here that I'll find that kind of solace. "I have to use the ladies' room."

Technically, I don't *have* to use it.

I'll go in and stand in a stall until I catch my breath and get over the initial shock of seeing West with another woman.

Why is it bothering me this much? He's a handsome man. It only makes sense that he'd be out on a Friday night with an attractive woman.

A woman he'll take home by the end of the night to fuck.

"I'll be right back," I spit out before Harmony has a chance to invite herself along.

I weave through the crowds, heading straight for the restrooms.

Once I reach the quiet corridor that leads to the ladies' room I breathe a sigh of relief and rest my back against the exposed brick wall.

I cover my face with my hands, willing myself to forget the image of West with the blonde.

"Angel? Are you alright?"

My hands drop. I turn my head to look at him standing next to me.

He's alone.

"West," I whisper his name; the name I called him that night in Vegas.

He takes one step closer, his eyes darkening. A ghost of a smile touches his lips. "It's about fucking time."

CHAPTER TWENTY-FOUR

FINALLY.

Linny Faye is finally admitting that she remembers what happened in Vegas. I have no idea if seeing the tiara pushed her to this point, or if it's the sheer weight of the constant denials.

She nervously looks past my shoulder to the end of the corridor. The restaurant beyond is bustling with people.

I saw her the second she walked in holding tight to the hand of the guy she was having dinner with the other night.

Roland. Fucking Roland.

"Were you with him when we fucked two months ago? Is that why you've been playing the amnesia game for so long?"

"I'm not playing a game." She straightens, her hands moving to smooth out the skirt of her dress. "And it's been days, West. It's only been a few days."

She's right, but it feels like weeks, longer if I'm honest.

"You didn't answer my question." I cross my arms over

my chest and look down at her. "Were you with Roland when we fucked?"

She's sexy as sin in the red dress she's got on. It's low cut enough that I am getting a perfect bird's eye view of the top of her breasts.

"How do you know his name?" She takes on the same defensive stance as me, but it only makes me want to touch her tits more. They're pressed together now above where she's crossed her arms.

"You two were having dinner here last Saturday."

"Oh my god, you've been following me." Her hands drop to her hips. "What the hell?"

I thought she was beautiful when she was beneath me, languid and serene after coming, but the way she looks right now takes it to an entirely new level.

She's hot as fuck when she's angry.

"I was having dinner with my business partner and thought I recognized you," I answer calmly, staring into her eyes. "I asked the server if he knew your name, but the only name he caught was your boyfriend's. Roland."

She gives her head a curt shake. "I can't believe this. You saw me before you walked into the conference room on Monday?"

"Were you sleeping with Roland when we fucked?" I press for an answer to *that* question because it's too damn important to ignore.

Her gaze searches my face for something. "I'm not like that. I would never cheat on a man."

Disappointment. That's what's swimming in her vivid green eyes. She's disappointed that I asked, that I assumed that she'd fuck one guy while another was waiting for her back in his bed.

"This is our second date." Her hand jumps to the center of her chest. "Tonight is the second time I've seen him."

Fuck. Just fuck.

She had her first date with him two days before I saw her in the conference room at Faye & Sons? I just missed my chance.

"Are you going to see him a third time?" I ask because I want Roland out of the picture.

"Linny?"

As if on cue, a guy's voice calls her name from behind me.

Roland's timing is impeccable, his taste in women too, but that won't stop me from shutting down whatever is happening between them.

"I'm here, Roland," she says loud enough that her soft voice carries through the long corridor.

"Is everything okay?" Heavy footsteps accompany the words.

Fuck this guy.

I lock eyes with her once more before I turn on my heel. He's headed straight for us.

"I'm fine," she says as she steps around me. "Mr. Weston and I were just talking business."

His hand is outstretched before he's in front of me. "Roland Elgar. It's good to meet you."

"Jeremy Weston." I take his hand in mine because being an asshole won't get me what I want. Charm will. "I was just about to invite Linny back to my table. I'd love if you both joined us."

"We're here with friends," he says, his hand dropping mine to grab hold of Linny's. He brings it to his lips and feathers a kiss over her knuckles. "We should get back to them."

"Stop by my table if you get a chance, Linny." I smile past the envy. I don't want his lips touching any part of her. "There's someone I'd like you to meet."

Her eyes narrow slightly. "I'm sure your date would prefer to have you all to herself tonight, Mr. Weston."

Jealousy looks even better on Linny than anger.

I want to push her against the brick wall, kiss her hard and fuck her even harder.

"You're talking about the blonde woman in the black dress?" I inch my brow up. "You noticed the two of us together?"

Her hand comes up to her hair, tugging on a strand. "She's lovely."

"I was talking about introducing you to my business partner, Rocco Jones." I ignore Roland and keep my gaze on her. "The woman I brought with me tonight is my cousin. Her name is Cindy."

The look on her pretty face is priceless. It's relief mixed with confusion.

"We should get back to Harmony and Reuben." Roland pulls on her hand. "It was good to meet you, Jeremy."

I can't say the same, so I don't say anything at all. The nod of my head does all the talking for me.

I watch them walk away, my gaze pinned to Linny's ass. I chuckle because I may not be going home with her tonight, but Roland isn't either.

The way she turns back to get one last glance at me is all the reassurance I need. She still wants me and now that we've established that we've fucked, it's only a matter of time until it happens again.

CHAPTER TWENTY-FIVE

LINNY

THE ONLY PRODUCTIVE thing I did all weekend was telling Roland that our second date was our last.

I couldn't bring myself to do it Friday night. I was emotionally exhausted from coming clean to West.

I knew that when I said his name, he'd take it as an admission. It was.

There were so many people at the Nova tasting party that after Roland and I left him in the corridor, I didn't see him again.

When it was time to leave, I told Roland I'd text him on Saturday. We said goodbye outside the restaurant the same way we did a week before. Our hug this time wasn't any less stilted or awkward.

Harmony watched from where she was standing a few feet away with Reuben.

Once she was back at her hotel for the night, she sent me

a text message telling me that she'd made a mistake thinking Roland was the guy for me.

On Saturday, over brunch at Crispy Biscuit, I told him that I thought we'd make better friends than lovers. He agreed with a confession.

Our first date at Nova was supposed to be his fifth date with another woman.

He'd made the reservation more than a month ago and when she broke off with him that afternoon, he asked Harmony to see if I was available.

We parted with the promise that we'd stay in touch, but it won't happen. I won't reach out, and I doubt Roland will either.

"You're here bright and early, Linny." My dad walks into my office with two cups of coffee in his hands. "I picked up your favorite from the café around the corner."

My dad still thinks I drink my coffee the same way I did back in high school, with five teaspoons of sugar and almost as much cream.

I've scaled it back since. I order it without anything added since all I'm really looking for each morning is a caffeine jolt.

I take the cup from his hand and sip it. I can almost feel my teeth decay as I swallow.

"How was your weekend, dad?"

He scrolls through the messages on his phone. It's his usual morning routine. He doesn't look at his phone until he's in the office, instead devoting the earliest moments of his day to his wife.

"We had dinner with some friends." He tips his head to the side. "Diane's friends. It was good."

He still makes the distinction, even though they've been married for years. They brought two lives together, complete with kids and homes. It's taken time for them both to adjust to their new normal of building a life together.

"I spoke to your sister yesterday." A smile blooms on his lips.

I did too. Bethy called me just as I was leaving the diner after saying goodbye to Roland. I saw no reason to mention him to her. I know my sister. She would have told me to turn back around and reconsider the relationship.

"I wish she'd come home," I say quietly. "I miss her."

It's not a lie. We may have fought with everything we had while we were growing up, but the last few years, we've become closer than ever. When she was offered a temporary position with a pharmaceutical company in Australia, she took it immediately.

My sister's passion is travel, so being handed the opportunity to spend a year on another continent was too good for her to pass up.

"I miss her too," he chimes in. "She'll be back when the time is right."

That may be never. She hopes to land a position in New Zealand once her current job wraps up.

I could use my saved vacation days and visit her, but that would give Mitchell an advantage. I need to keep my feet firmly planted in Manhattan until my dad makes a decision about the next CEO of Faye & Sons.

"What's on your agenda today?" I ask before I take another sip of the sugary sweet lukewarm coffee.

"Mitchell and I are meeting with a potential new client." He doesn't look up from his phone. "It's one of the major players in footwear."

My mouth drops. I've been waiting for that call for months, and I've somehow been left out of the introductory meeting.

I'm the one who stalked the owner to pitch our ideas for their upcoming winter boot campaign.

"I'll clear my schedule so I can be there," I offer with a smile.

He finally looks up, his eyes bright. "No need, sweetheart. Your brother and I can handle it."

My stomach knots the way it always does when he refers to Mitchell that way. I don't consider him my brother.

He's a guy who is gunning for the same promotion as me, and it sounds like he's taking things to a new level.

"I want you to sit down with Trent and Jeremy and go over their campaign." He picks up his coffee cup before he darts to his feet. "Why don't you call Rizon and set up a meeting for later today? I'd like an update by tomorrow morning on where things stand with that account."

I'd like an update on where his head is at regarding the CEO position.

I studied marketing because I expected to take over the family business one day. I never imagined that the only child of his second wife would swoop in and threaten that.

"I'll take care of it." I paste on a smile. "If you need anything for your meeting let me know."

Translation: I can be in the conference room in thirty seconds flat. Ten if I kick off my heels and sprint.

He leaves my office without so much as another word.

I pick up my phone and text a message to Trent.

Linny: *Are you available for lunch? Let's meet and go over the campaign.*

His reply takes less than a minute.

Trent: *Spent the weekend with my brother's family. Six kids. All with the flu. I'm stuck in bed. I'll set up something for you and Jeremy at noon. Details to follow.*

I drop my head onto my desk, resting my forehead against the wood.

Great.

That conversation West and I started to have in the corridor at Nova is about to continue over lunch today.

My Monday just went from bad to worse.

CHAPTER TWENTY-SIX

JEREMY

MY MONDAY just went from decent to fucking spectacular.

Trent's text message telling me that he was sick shouldn't have been the best news I've heard all day, but it was.

Linny Faye wants a meeting with my Brand Manager and since he's stuck flat on his back in bed, I'm stepping in.

I arranged for lunch to be delivered because I want her alone now that she's finally dropped the façade and admitted that my cock was inside of her two months ago.

A knock on my office door draws me to my feet. I straighten my gray tie and button my navy blue suit jacket.

"Come in."

The door swings open and Blythe steps in. "See what I did there? I knocked."

I fold my arms across my chest. "It's about time. What do you want?"

"You get right to the point, don't you?"

"I pay you to get to the point, so what is it?" I roll my hand in the air to move the conversation forward.

She eyes my desk. "I ordered lunch for you and Ms. Faye. It will be delivered and served in conference room A. Your plan was to have that poor woman eat lunch at your desk, right?"

Wrong. I want to eat that woman on my desk. The catered lunch is a polite gesture. If I had my way, I would be feasting on her pussy as my main course.

I just need to remove Roland from the equation before I dive between her legs. I won't touch a woman who is fucking another man.

That's a hard limit for me.

"Take an extra hour for lunch today, Blythe."

She perks one brow. "Why?"

"Because today I'm a kind son-of-a-bitch who wants his assistant to treat herself to a nice lunch."

She glances back over her shoulder at her desk. "Something isn't adding up here. You're going to pack up my stuff while I'm gone, aren't you? I'm about to get fired because of the raise I gave myself."

What the fuck?

"How much?" I lean back against my desk.

I don't have time for this shit right now. I should reprimand her, but whatever amount she's banking still isn't enough. We both know it.

"Enough," she answers with a smile. "You still make more than me."

"I sure as hell hope I do." I laugh.

"Excuse me?"

Blythe turns at the sound of the feminine voice behind her. "Hello, Ms. Faye."

"Come in, Linny. I've been expecting you." I take a measured step closer to the doorway. Closer to her.

Blythe moves to the side and I get an eyeful.

Linny is dressed in a navy blue wraparound dress that hugs her curves and accentuates every part of her gorgeous body.

She turns to look at Blythe. "Will you be joining us?"

"No." I toss back. "Blythe is leaving. It's just you and me, Linny."

Her chest heaves and my gaze is drawn to her nipples. They've furled into tight points under her dress.

"Close the door on your way out," I call after Blythe.

She does, leaving me alone with the woman I've desperately wanted since she left my bed in Las Vegas.

———

LINNY TAKES a seat in one of the chairs in front of my desk and slides a notepad and a pen from her bag. "I thought we could start with the guest list for the launch party."

I lower myself into the chair next to her since she's made herself at home. "Put the notepad away."

She shakes her head softly. "I need to take notes. I prefer writing them out by hand as opposed to saving them to a tablet. I know it's old-fashioned, but it works best for me."

I ignore all of that because I didn't hear the name *Roland* yet. I need to hear that name one last time in the context that he's gone to hell and won't be coming back.

My jaw clenches. "Tell me you dumped him."

She takes a deep breath. "Who?"

"Who the hell do you think?"

She looks at me, her eyes narrowed. "Are you asking me if I dumped Roland?"

"Yes," I answer succinctly. "Did you dump him?"

"That's a highly inappropriate question to ask me during a business meeting."

I reach forward to snatch the notepad from her hands.

She gasps when I toss it onto my desk.

I watch her carefully. "Our business meeting is over."

"I can't do this, " she says through a ragged breath. "We have to forget about what happened in Vegas."

"Why?" Tension grips my shoulders. I reach back to squeeze my neck, warding off the stress headache I know is about to bear down on me.

Her hands shake. "I can't have anything to do with you right now, West."

"Because of Roland?" I draw his name into two long syllables. "Dump him, Linny. He's not right for you."

"You don't know me." She turns in her seat to face me. "We spoke on an airplane for a total of ten minutes and then we fucked. Once."

Technically, she's right, but I feel connected to her in a way that can't be measured in minutes or seconds. It surpasses that. It makes no sense, but I know that she feels it too.

"It was special," I say the words even though I know they sound cliché. "I told you I've thought about you daily since then. I wasn't lying."

"It's not as simple as that." Her hand goes to her forehead. "It's complicated, West."

"It's not," I argue. I never argue with women over this shit. If one decides she's had enough of me, I move on. The same is true if I'm tired of a woman. I'll say my goodbyes, wish them well, and forget about them.

That hasn't happened yet with Linny. I haven't stopped

thinking about her since we were together in Vegas. I don't know how to handle that.

"Dump Roland, have dinner with me and take me home with you." I lean closer to her. "It's as simple as that."

She shifts in her seat, pulling back from me. "I dumped him on Saturday."

Thank Christ.

"That doesn't mean anything can happen between us." She's quick to add. "We have to forget about Vegas. This needs to be strictly professional."

"We're past that." I rest my palms on my knees. "You can't tell me that you're not feeling the same pull to me as I am to you."

She closes her eyes briefly, her neck craning back. "West."

My name comes out of her soft lips like a plea, a wish, a needy request.

"Linny," I whisper. "Just let yourself feel. We were good together that night. We can have more of that."

"We can't." Her eyes fly open and lock on mine. "If I sleep with you again, I'll lose everything."

CHAPTER TWENTY-SEVEN

LINNY

THAT WAS MELODRAMATIC. That's not who I am, but every word is true.

West is rubbing his temples. He hasn't said anything in response to my declaration that I can't sleep with him again.

I owe him more of an explanation than what I've given considering I just spent almost an entire week pretending I didn't know him.

"West?" I say his name softly. "I'm sorry."

He looks down, avoiding eye contact with me. "For what?"

I want to reach out and touch his shoulder, but if I do that, I'll feel that same addictive rush of electricity that charged through my body that night in Las Vegas.

I rest my hands in my lap, clasping them tightly together to try and mask how badly they're shaking.

"I was wrong when I pretended not to know you," I say the words that I should have said a week ago.

He finally looks at me, his expression impassive. "Why did you do it?"

I wish the answer were concise and straightforward, but it's complicated, so I go right to the core of the issue.

"Faye & Sons has a strict policy about employees having sex with clients. It's not allowed."

His brows perk. "I'll hire another firm to work on the campaign. You're fired."

I can't tell if he's joking or not, so I laugh. "You don't mean that."

He skips past that to ask me a question. "We fucked months ago, Linny. You can't get in shit for that, can you?"

Technically, no, but if my dad knew about it, I would have been excluded from the Rizon campaign altogether which would have been another notch in Mitchell's belt.

There's more to it than that, but it's personal and I don't know West well enough to bare my soul to him.

"My dad is retiring next year and I'm up for the position of CEO when he does." I pause to consider my next words. "Mitchell is a candidate too, so every action counts right now."

West's gaze scans my face. He studies me carefully. "You were worried that your dad would be disappointed in you for fucking a stranger. That's it, isn't it?"

I swallow hard, my throat chalky and dry. I'm twenty-six-years-old. I should be able to make my own choices, and mistakes. I want to and need to, but as long as I'm fighting Mitchell for my dream job, my dad's opinion still matters.

"That's part of it," I answer honestly. "I'm trying not to give Mitchell ammunition that he can use against me."

West's hand drifts to the armrest of my chair. I stare down at it. It's large and I know I'll find comfort in it. I want to reach for it, but I stop myself.

"Why the fuck is Mitchell up for the job?" His jaw tight-ens. "He's not a Faye, is he?"

I shake my head and sigh. "His mom married my dad a few years ago."

"He's your stepbrother?"

I lean back in the chair. "He's my competition."

He nods knowingly. "I see what's happening here. Dear old dad has pitted the two of you against each other in a death match. Whoever is left standing at the end, gets to take over the company."

"In a nutshell, that's about right." I half-shrug. "You would think since the company bears my surname, that I'd have an advantage, but that's not the case."

"Do you have any brothers?"

I straighten. "Just me and my sister."

"Where did the Faye & Son's name come from?" He turns in his chair, so he's facing me directly now.

"My grandfather wanted his sons to work with him. One did." I wave one finger in the air. "My dad. He hoped to have a son or two to keep that legacy alive."

His eyes narrow. "Your grandfather was Lincoln Faye? I saw his portrait hanging in the reception area when I came to your offices."

"I'm his namesake." Bringing my hand to my lips, I sigh. "There were complications during my birth. The doctors told my parents that my mother would never be able to carry another child, so my dad insisted on naming me himself. He always wanted a son, so he named me after his father."

A flicker of something washes over his expression. It's not pity and I'm grateful for that. I felt sorry for myself for years when my dad would joke about how I was supposed to be a boy. I always knew that he loved me, but it stung and bearing the name of my grandfather is a constant reminder of who I will never be.

"Your name is beautiful." He gazes into my eyes. "Everything about you is beautiful."

It would be so easy to lean forward to kiss him.

"You want to make your father proud." He pauses for a minute and then continues, "I get that."

It's an invitation for me to ask about his family, but that's not my business. I can't open any door that will take me a step closer to him. "I want the CEO position. It's not just because the first thing I'll do is fire Mitchell."

That pulls a hearty laugh from him. "That guy is an asshole."

"You have no idea."

He reaches to touch my hand and I don't stop him, even though I know I should pull back.

"I understand discretion." He brings my hand to his lips, resting it there, as he goes on. "We can be together and keep our business relationship separate."

It's so tempting. The thought of being in his arms again sends a shiver of desire up my spine.

"It was good that night," he growls as his eyes scan my body. "Jesus, Linny, it was so fucking good. You can't deny that."

He's right. I can't. "It was good."

"The best you've ever had." His brow lifts.

I smile at his arrogance. "Was it the best you've ever had?"

He presses my fingers to his lips and closes his eyes. "By far. I've come so many times thinking about fucking you. I ache for you."

I feel lightheaded. His words offer me something I didn't know I was craving.

It's surreal that a man I only spent a few hours with could feel the same things for me that I feel for him. Doubt seeps in so I ask the question that's been on the tip of my tongue for days. "When you first saw me in the conference room last week, what did you think?"

His eyes meet mine. "I felt like I won the lottery."

CHAPTER TWENTY-EIGHT

JEREMY

HER CHEEKS FLUSH.

She looks down, hiding her reaction to my words, but it's too late. I know she felt the same way when she saw me standing in the conference room last week.

"It looks like we're at an impasse," I say to lure her gaze back up.

It works. "An impasse? How so?"

I trail her fingertips over my lips before I kiss them one last time. I slip my hand from hers and I hear it. I hear the slightest sigh of regret at the loss of my touch.

"It's against the rules to fuck me." I don't mince words because there's no need. "You won't let me fire you."

A soft smile slides over her perfect mouth. "I suppose you could call that an impasse."

"You want me, angel."

"Yes," she whispers, the nod of her head confirming her words. "You know that I do."

"Tell me how to make this work." I edge closer to her in my chair. "We can be discreet. We'll meet at a hotel, or here. You name the place and time and I'll be there, with a believable work excuse in my back pocket in the event anyone ever questions you about where you are."

Her gaze drops to my pants and the bulge that I gave up trying to hide. "You're talking about finding a place to fuck, aren't you?"

"A place where we can spend time together without the threat of exposure," I clarify.

She ponders that with a sweep of her hand over her forehead. "You're suggesting that we meet to fuck under the guise that we're conducting business."

Hearing her say the word *fuck* over and over is making everything fall away but my need to feel her, taste her and be inside her beautiful body.

"I'm suggesting that we fuck, soon, and we can do that wherever the hell you want." I jerk my thumb toward my desk. "I'll eat you right now on my desk. I'll fuck you bent over it. I don't care where I have you. I just want you."

Her fingers trace a path over her jaw before they whisper over the skin of her neck, drawing lazy circles.

I don't even know if she's aware of how erotic she looks like right now.

"Your assistant would hear us." She laughs like she thinks I was trying to be funny.

I correct that with one sentence. "I'm serious, Linny."

"You're not serious," she counters. "We can't have sex in your office."

I push to stand, holding a hand out to her. "Get on my desk."

She swats my hand away with a brush of hers. "No, West. I don't do that."

"You also don't fuck men you just met. Yet, you fucked me. I want you right now."

She peers over her shoulder. "Your assistant could come back at any moment."

I glance down at my watch. "She won't and even if she did, she'd know to hold my calls when she heard you screaming my name."

She pushes to her feet. "I wouldn't scream your name."

"You did in Vegas."

Her feet shuffle to the side to gain distance from me. I don't give in. I follow every step of hers with one of my own.

"I had a little too much to drink that night." She tugs on the front of her dress. "Any other night, I wouldn't have done it."

She starts walking backward toward the door of my office. I stalk her, shrugging out of my suit jacket. I toss it back onto the chair she was just sitting in.

"Why are you taking off your jacket?"

"It's hot in here." I loosen my tie. "You look flushed."

Her hand darts to her cheek. "I don't. I'm not."

She stops dead when her back hits my closed office door. Her hand searches for the doorknob, but I'm on her before she can turn it.

I reach down and lock it. "Tell me you want to leave."

Her head shakes back and forth. "I should leave."

"Do you want to leave?" My arms bracket her, my palms pressing against the door on either side of her head. "Tell me you want to leave and I'll let you go."

"I have meetings, I think." Her eyes lock on mine. "I think I have other work to do today."

I lean closer, breathing in the scent of her. That perfume. I haven't smelled it since that night; since I had my lips wrapped around her nipple. "God, you smell incredible."

"You do too," she says softly.

"I'll never forget our first kiss. Let me kiss you again." My voice is laced with need. "Just one kiss."

"One kiss," she repeats back in a whisper. Her tongue darts out to slick her bottom lip. "Only one kiss, West."

I slide my hand to her neck, tilting her head to just the right angle. "If it's just one, I need to make it count."

I do.

CHAPTER TWENTY-NINE

LINNY

HIS KISS IS everything I remember from that night in Vegas, and more.

It's tender, soft, and yet, there's just enough want in it to make my knees weak.

I weave my fingers through his hair and it pulls a deep groan from him.

My sex clenches at the sound of the desire in it and in the hunger that's in his touch.

One of his hands is cradling my cheek. The other has started a journey down my neck, to my shoulder before it brushes the side of my left breast.

He pushes himself against me, forcing my back against the door.

I can feel every hard plane of his body and the rigid length of his cock through his pants.

"I need to taste you." His breath breezes over my cheek. "Now."

I shake my head, even though every cell in my body is yearning for more. "We can't."

"We can." His tongue trails a slow path over my bottom lip before he tugs it between his teeth.

I moan at the burst of pain and the reminder that I did the same to him in Vegas. "Your assistant."

His hand moves lower, skimming over the fabric of my dress until he reaches the sash. "She's not here."

"West," I manage to whisper his name when he tugs on the sash to open my dress.

His gaze drops to take in the sight of my black lace panties and bra. "Jesus, Linny. Look at you."

I do. I look down and my breath hitches.

Everything slows when his hand glides a path over my panties before he dips a finger inside. "You're so fucking wet. I've been craving a taste of this for two months straight."

"You haven't," I counter with a hand on his shoulder. "A man like you doesn't remember a random one-night stand."

His lips are on mine again, this time his kiss is rough and demanding. His eyes bore into me when he pulls back. "I remember everything about that night. Every single fucking detail right down to the mole on your left shoulder."

My gaze darts to my shoulder, but my dress covers the mole.

"I haven't touched another woman since I was with you." His lips slide over my chin toward my neck. "I haven't wanted another woman since you."

I close my eyes against the weight of those words.

He hasn't been with anyone else. I haven't been with anyone else.

He exhales sharply. "Tell me to stop now, angel, or relax and enjoy the ride."

"Don't stop," I whisper into the still air of his office. "Please, don't."

I look down when he drops to his knees, his breath skimming my stomach before his lips find my thigh. Time slows when he slides my panties to the side to expose me.

"You're so beautiful." His voice is low and rough, filled with raw need. "Every part of you is breathtaking, Linny."

I shield my face with my forearm, biting my bottom lip to try and quell the uncontrollable desire to moan.

I do just that when the tip of his tongue snakes over my folds. "Such a sweet pussy. So sweet."

I've never been with a man who talked to me during sex. My lovers have always been the selfish and silent type. They'd touch or lick me briefly before taking what they wanted.

"West, please," I whimper when he inches back to blow over my core. "I'm so ready."

"You'll come the second I suck on your clit." He rubs his fingertip over it.

It spurs me closer to an orgasm. I'm so close to the edge already. "Please."

I don't want to beg. I want to come.

One of his hands glides over my hip until it cups my ass. "Put your leg over my shoulder."

I do without thinking. I don't care what I look like. All I want is to feel.

He glances up at me, his dark eyes swimming with desire. "I've thought about this for two months. Craved this. I've fucking ached for this."

I lace my fingers through his soft brown hair and tug him closer to me.

"I'll give you everything you want." He licks the length of my cleft. "And everything you need."

My back arches when he licks me over and over, his tongue diving into me before he circles my clit.

It's too much. It's all too intense. Words fall from my lips that I can't recognize. His name becomes a chant as I buck against his face, riding him shamelessly, my back hitting the door in a pounding rhythm.

He sucks on my clit, the pressure perfect, the sounds he makes my undoing.

I moan again, louder this time as I race to the edge.

He slides a thick finger inside me and hones in on the spot that sends me into a withering frenzy.

I push against him to stop the pleasure. It's too much. It's all so much, but he's relentless.

He hums against my tender flesh, sucking, tasting, biting, taking.

I come so hard that I hold both hands over my mouth to buffer the scream.

"Again, angel."

Two words that take me from one orgasm straight into another with his name falling in a whispered plea from my lips.

CHAPTER THIRTY

JEREMY

I GLIDE UP HER BODY, feathering kisses over her skin. She smells like heaven. The taste of her is intoxicating.

"Linny," I whisper her name against her lips. "Open your eyes."

She shakes her head softly. "I can't. I can't move anything."

Pressing my mouth against hers for a kiss, I laugh. "You can. Open them."

She does.

A smile parts her lips. "I came here to talk business."

Wrapping my arm around her waist, I chuckle. "You're not complaining, are you? That was a hell of a lot better than talking about vodka."

Her hand finds my cheek. "So much better."

I lick my bottom lip to savor the lingering taste of her. "That was incredible. I need to do that again."

Her back bows against the door. "I won't be able to function."

I want to fuck her so badly, but I don't have protection here.

I gave up carrying condoms in my pocket or wallet after I turned down a handful of women who were willing to hop into bed with me.

Eventually, I would have shaken my obsession with my Vegas angel, but only in an attempt to satisfy a physical need, not because of any connection beyond that.

It would have been sex, pure and simple.

What I just shared with Linny is more; so much more.

Her hand skims the front of my pants. "Would you let me... I want to…"

I've been hard since she arrived at my office, but the suggestion of her dropping to her knees to blow me is almost too much.

I groan loudly before I claim her mouth for a soft kiss. "You want to suck me off."

It's not a question or a demand. It's a desire that she feels and is struggling to express vocally, although her hand is clear in its intention. It's on my belt buckle.

"Yes," she whispers as she leans her forehead against my cheek. "I almost did it in Vegas. I thought about waking you up that way."

My hand falls to cover hers on my belt buckle. "Fuck. You should have. I woke up hard and aching for you, but you were gone."

She leans back to look up, her eyes catching mine. "I had to catch a flight."

I have a dozen responses for that including the obvious one. She could have booked a later flight and stayed in my bed.

"You'll make it up to me now." I reach down to unbuckle my belt, willing myself to calm the fuck down, so I don't shoot my load all over her face the second her wet lips touch my dick.

She nods, but then time stops. Every fucking thing stops because of a knock on my office door.

———

WHOEVER THE FUCK it is knocks a second time.

"What?" I call out, a frustrated edge to my tone.

"Jeremy?"

The voice is vaguely familiar and annoying as hell. Mitchell. Goddamn Mitchell Bilton is standing on the other side of my closed office door.

"It's Mitchell," he confirms what I already know.

Judging by the look of terror on Linny's face she recognizes her asshole of a stepbrother's voice too.

I press a finger to her lips to silence her. Clearing my throat I call out, "I'm busy. What do you want?"

The door handle rattles. The asshole is trying to get in. "Is Linny in there?"

I kiss her softly, wanting to ease the panic that I see washing over her expression.

"Her assistant told me she had a meeting with you." His voice lowers. "I should have been included in that."

"I would have asked you to accompany her if I thought that was necessary." I roll my eyes, luring a smile to Linny's lips.

I hear rustling outside the door before he clears his throat. "Alright. I'm here now. Do you want to grab a beer? My treat."

Linny's brows jump.

"He's a persistent bastard," I whisper against her ear.

She nods, a soft smile touching her mouth.

"I'm busy, Mitchell." I slide a hand over her leg, drawing a soft gasp from her. "Go back to your office. We'll talk tomorrow."

"I'll wait." His voice drifts farther away. "I'll sit out here and wait until you're done. I have some ideas to throw at you."

"Oh my god." Linny's hands fist the front of my shirt. "He's going to see me in here. He'll know what we just did. Is there a back way out of your office?"

I brush my lips against hers. "I'll handle it. You're not crawling out of a window. It would be hell trying to repel thirty-six floors down the side of the building in those heels."

Her hand darts to her mouth to silence her laugh.

"I'll let him buy me a drink. One shot of vodka." I make quick work of my belt. "You stay here until the coast is clear."

"*I'm sorry*," she mouths, her chin dipping toward the sizable bulge in my pants.

I shrug into my suit jacket. "Next time, angel. There will be a next time. Soon."

I kiss her one last time before I open my office door just wide enough that I can slip through without the risk of Mitchell catching a glimpse of what's inside.

CHAPTER THIRTY-ONE

LINNY

"HEY LINNY, I spent the last few hours with Jeremy Weston."

I look up to see Mitchell standing in the open doorway of my office with a smug grin on his face.

I glance down at the small silver clock that sits on the corner of my desk. It's one of the few things I inherited from my granddad. "Isn't it past your bedtime?"

His gaze drops to his watch. "It's not even five p.m."

"Dad told me that you like to get in your jammies and watch Netflix before dinner."

His face reddens. "I did that once when I was sick. He stopped by my place with chicken soup."

That sounds like my dad. He's been my hero all of my life. I'm not surprised that he'd step up to become Mitchell's too since his own father took off before he was born.

"What did you and Jeremy talk about this afternoon?" He takes it upon himself to walk into my office so he can plop down in one of the white leather chairs in front of my desk.

"Make yourself at home," I say sarcastically.

My tone is lost on him since his gaze is glued to the screen of his phone. "Dave put me in charge of the Vrite Footwear campaign."

I paste a smile on my face even though I'm seething inside. I worked hard to land that account and now it's in Mitchell's incompetent hands.

My silence lures his gaze back up. "It pisses you off, doesn't it?"

"What?" I ask casually.

"That I'm in charge of that account." He taps the back of his phone case on the edge of my desk. "That I'm up for the promotion. That you're going to have to answer to me in a few months."

I'm mostly pissed off that I've worked hard for years, devoting myself to the family business at every turn and it may have all been a waste of time. There's a strong possibility that I'll be passed over to lead it.

Mitchell doesn't let up. "That I'm the son your dad always wanted."

That one stings. He knows it, but I refuse to show it.

"What are your plans for the Vrite campaign?" I shoot him a look, knowing that he won't have an answer.

"What are your plans for the Rizon launch party?" he counters with a sneer. "Jeremy said that you were still working out the small details. You should get a move on, don't you think?"

You should go to hell.

The words play on my tongue until I catch sight of my dad. He's headed straight toward my office with a wide grin on his face.

"We got the house," he announces as he strolls through the doorway. "Your mother and I have our Florida homestead and we can't wait to move."

She's not my mother, but he is my father.

I push to my feet and round my desk to hug him.

It's inevitable now. There won't be a reprieve. He's moving to Florida and one way or another, my life will change forever.

———

I GLANCE down at my phone one last time before I reach for the remote to turn off the television in my bedroom.

I got home about an hour ago. It was after eleven. I'd spent the evening with my dad. We had dinner and toasted to his upcoming move.

He did almost all of the talking, exuberance driving his every word.

I've never seen him this happy and each time I snuck a peek at my phone, I half expected to look up to see disappointment on his face.

In his perfect world, all phones would be turned off during dinner, but I wasn't playing by that rule tonight.

West texted me after I left his office this afternoon.

He promised that if he had the time, he'd call me tonight.

My phone has been silent all night except for a few text messages from Harmony and an email from Ivy about lunch later in the week.

Resting my back against my headboard, I slide my laptop onto my lap and flip it open.

My fingers hover over the keyboard before I type his name into the search bar.

Jeremy Weston.

This time I avoid all images and zero in on the Rizon company website.

His bio is generic. It's nothing more than some disjointed facts about his education and his familial connection to the company's founder.

I go back to the search results and skim them, looking for something more.

Nothing catches my eye once I realize that the man doesn't have any social media accounts.

I move to shut the laptop but stop myself.

I take a deep breath and with shaking hands, I type in my name.

Lincoln Walsh.

I relcase the breath once I realize that virtually every result on the first page is focused on my grandfather. The second page too and the third.

I hit the backspace button again and again until the search bar is blank.

Linny Walsh.

I stare at my nickname after typing it out.

"Please don't be there," I whisper to myself as I hit the enter button. "Please."

My heart hammers as I scan each result.

My bio page on the Faye & Sons' website pops up. My social media accounts take up the next four spots.

There are quotes that clients have made and an old magazine article that features a picture of Clive Parker, the head of Corteck, a software company that hired me to help them launch a series of new apps two years ago, and me.

I read every result; page after page of generic work-related material is all I find.

Snapping the cover of my laptop shut, I breathe a sigh of relief. My biggest mistake hasn't found its way online. I pray that it never does.

CHAPTER THIRTY-TWO

JEREMY

"YOU'RE MORE creative than you look."

A smile plays on my lips as I stare across the table at Linny. "Is that a compliment?"

She shrugs and finishes the last sip of wine from her glass. "That's for you to decide."

We've been sitting at this table in a bistro on the Upper West Side for the past hour. I ordered for us both when I arrived. She dove into the steak salad with gusto, complimenting me on my good taste.

I told her to eat it all since I plan on using up every ounce of her energy at the hotel around the corner once she agrees to join me there.

"I'll take it as intended." I drink from the glass of ice water the server has already refilled twice for me. "You don't view me as the creative type, but you're impressed by my creativity as it relates to my plan for us to fuck."

Her brows lift at the last word. "Is that why you called

this meeting? So you can tempt me with steak and wine before you strip me naked?"

I'd agree immediately except that the pale pink sweater dress she has on is the hottest thing I've seen her in, save for the tank top and tutu.

A vision of her in that dress on her knees with my cock sliding between her lips has been floating through my mind since she walked into the bistro.

I lean my forearms on the table and drop my voice to a low whisper. "We're going to spend all afternoon fucking each other at the hotel around the corner."

Her gaze drifts to the door of the bistro. "Are you taking me to a hotel instead of your place because you're worried someone will spot us?"

That should be the reason, but it's not.

I can't take her to my apartment. Explaining why is a conversation for another time, another day, preferably when whatever is happening between us has a foundation that's rooted in more than an undeniable attraction and phenomenal sex.

"We could go to my place, but Mitchell drops by there sometimes to annoy the hell out of me." She rolls her eyes. "I never invite him over but that hasn't stopped him from showing up unannounced."

"When did your dad marry his mom?"

My question surprises her. I see it in the slowing of her hand as she lifts the napkin from the table to bring it to her mouth. "It's been about seven years now."

"Were you happy for them?" I ask, searching her face for any sign that this subject is making her uncomfortable. The only thing I see is quiet resignation.

She nods. "After my parents divorced, I wanted them to be happy. For the first couple of years I wanted them to do that together, but once I realized that would never happen, I was rooting for them both to find love again."

It's a mature approach to a fucked up situation.

"Did your mom find love again?"

A soft smile tugs at her lips. "She's still looking, but she's having a lot of fun figuring that out."

"Tell me about your sister." I lean back in the chair and cross my arms over my chest. "What's she like?"

"Bethy?" Her entire face brightens. "She's bold and smart. Bethy is blonde, blue-eyed. She's the spitting image of my mom."

I stumbled across a picture of Bethy online when I was searching for anything I could find about Linny. There wasn't much but an image posted to Linny's Instagram account four months ago caught my eye.

Linny was standing next to a blonde woman. They had their arms wrapped around each other's shoulders. They looked nothing alike, but their bond was obvious. The tag in the caption took me to Bethy's page.

She's attractive, but in my eyes, she doesn't hold a candle to Linny.

"What about your family?" she asks with a grin. "All I know is that you inherited the business from your granddad. There must be more to your story."

She has no idea.

My eyes drift over her shoulder.

"You have to be fucking kidding me."

Her napkin snaps out of her hand and hits the table. "Jesus, West. It was just a question."

I shake my head, holding my hand in the air. "No, angel. That comment wasn't for you."

She glances back over her shoulder. "Isn't that..."

I drop my napkin on the table and rise to my feet. "That's

my assistant. Something tells me I'm not going to like what she has to say."

———

AFTER BLYTHE TAKES a seat at the table, I scrub my hand over my face. "How did you find me?"

She taps the screen of the phone in her hand. "I put that tracking app back on your phone yesterday."

Linny smiles. "You track his phone?"

Blythe nods, glancing at me. "He disappears from the office sometimes without leaving word where he's going. If an emergency pops us, I need to know where he is."

Confusion mars Linny's expression. She doesn't say anything, but I see the question in her eyes. She's wondering if I abandon work to fuck other women during the day.

I haven't. Ever. Work has always trumped pleasure, until now.

"You weren't answering your phone." Blythe gestures to where my phone is sitting on the table. I turned it off when I got to the bistro to avoid being interrupted. "I wouldn't have hiked across town if it wasn't an urgent matter."

She looks to Linny and I can tell that she's silently wondering if this conversation should be private.

I have no fucking idea if it should, so I ask.

"What is this about, Blythe?"

She nervously picks at a crumb on the tablecloth. "Trent."

Linny pushes back from the table. "I need to use the ladies' room."

My plan all day was to spend the afternoon inside of her. That's being shot to hell right now, apparently because Trent has fucked something up.

The temptation to fire him is reaching its breaking point.

I stand when Linny does. "Our meeting for this afternoon is still on."

Her eyes meet mine. "Hear Blythe out and then we can discuss that."

Goddammit. I don't want anything to come between us today.

I drop back into my chair when Linny rounds the corner toward the restrooms. "Spit it out. What the hell is going on with Trent?"

She peers around the bistro before she turns back to me and lowers her voice. "Nothing. It's not about Trent. It's Athena. There's been an accident."

CHAPTER THIRTY-THREE

LINNY

I REST my head back and close my eyes, again. If this isn't heaven, I don't know what is.

It's past dusk now and I'm in a claw foot tub that's filled with warm water and fragrant bubbles.

The most magnificent view of New York City is to my left.

I arrived at this luxury hotel on Central Park West three hours ago.

West slid the key card to me this afternoon at the bistro after he told me that he had something urgent to take care of.

He whispered that he hoped I'd stay at the hotel tonight. My answer was simple. I told him that I would as long as he joined me.

I haven't heard a word from him since he said a brusque goodbye to me and left the bistro to join Blythe who was waiting for him on the sidewalk outside.

After focusing on work for the afternoon, I went home to

pack an overnight bag before I grabbed an Uber and headed back uptown.

I've used my time here wisely, ordering a delicious dinner from room service before diving into a phone meeting with Ivy.

My apartment is cozy, lovely and all mine, but it can't compete with this place.

The solace of not hearing the people who live above me walk around on the creaky floors is enough of an incentive for me to stay.

I'll sleep well tonight unless West shows up. If he does, I'll be well fucked. I'll take that over sleep any night of the week.

I smile when I hear the sound of the door to the suite opening.

Heavy footsteps cross the floor of the main living area before they slow as they near the bedroom.

I'm tucked away in the en suite bathroom with its stunning gray marble and silver accents.

"I've never seen anything more beautiful than this."

I open my eyes and turn my head at the sound of West's voice. "You made it."

His suit jacket is on the floor. His hands make quick work of his tie and his shirt. Both land in a heap next to the jacket as he toes out of his black shoes. "I'm sorry it took so long. I wanted to be here hours ago."

I watch as he pushes down his pants and boxers, his thick cock curving up toward his navel. He slides his hand over it, a quick brush of skin against skin.

"You're here now." I glide my fingers through the water. "I think there's room for two."

Before I met West, I never would have invited a man to join me in the bath. If I happened to spend the night with a guy, I'd lock the bathroom door before I showered in the morning.

I don't recognize who I am when I'm with him. I'm comfortable in a way I haven't been before and I like it.

He steps into the tub, settling in across from me.

"I wasn't sure if you'd be here." His hand rakes through his hair. "I know you're risking a lot to be with me."

Guilt nips at me. I'm breaking the rules. I'm putting my future at stake because I want this man more than I've wanted anything.

"I don't want to think about that." I reach out a hand to him. "Let's enjoy tonight."

That I can do." He takes my hand in his, pulling me closer. "Come here, angel."

I slide into his lap until our lips meet for a soft kiss.

His strong arms circle me. "Can I just stare at you for an hour or two?"

My hand runs over my damp hair. My makeup is washed away. My skin flushed from the heat in the water. "I'm a mess."

His eyes search mine. "I thought I knew what beauty was until I saw you on the airplane. You're even more breath-taking tonight."

I run the pad of my thumb over his left brow, smoothing it. "You mean that, don't you? They're not just words to you?"

His hands leap to my face, cupping my cheeks. "My grandfather lost his sight a few years before he died."

The emotion in his words catches me off guard. I fumble with what to say in response, so I sit in silence staring into his deep brown eyes.

"He knew it was coming, and the man was stoic as shit." He lets out a deep laugh.

I can't help but smile. "He sounds very strong."

"He was." He dips his chin. "I only saw him cry once. Just one time."

"When?" I whisper.

He takes a deep breath. "When he realized that he'd never see my grandma's face again."

I swallow hard, biting back a wave of unexpected emotion. "That's beautiful and incredibly sad. He must have loved her very much."

His gaze searches my face before he glances to the left and the vast view of the city beyond the glass of the window. "He loved her with everything he had. He died holding tightly to her hand."

I don't stop him when his hand slides from my face to my shoulder and down to my waist. He grips my bare skin, tugging me closer to him.

"He told me to appreciate beauty in its purest form every chance I could." His tongue slicks his bottom lip. "I do that each time I look at you."

I rest my hands on his chest and lean in to kiss him on the lips. "I'm glad I'm here."

He brushes his fingertips over my chin. "Me too, angel."

CHAPTER THIRTY-FOUR

JEREMY

I THREAD my fingers through Linny's hair, straining to control each of her movements.

My cock is between her lips. Her tongue is circling the tip and all I want to do is fuck her mouth. The desire to hold her in place and pump into her is all consuming.

Sweat peppers every inch of my skin as I fight the urge to hold her head in place and take what I want.

I did that after our bath.

I picked her up after toweling her off, dropped her in the middle of the bed and settled between her thighs.

I ate her pussy until she begged me to stop. I didn't. I finally slid my mouth up her body when she cried out that she couldn't take it anymore.

I couldn't either. My cock was aching. When I fell onto my back, she was on top of me in an instant.

"I won't come in your mouth," I growl the words out through clenched teeth. "I want to come inside of you."

She shakes her head, her tongue stroking a lazy path over the head of my dick.

I tighten my grip on her hair, giving it a gentle pull. "If you don't stop, I'll fuck your mouth."

Her brow lifts to accept the challenge. Her hand strokes the length of me, faster, harder.

I groan in response and she moans. She fucking moans around my cock and I'm gone.

I grip both hands in her hair and thrust up while I push her head down. I pump into her mouth with deep, steady drives.

She takes it all, teetering on her knees on the bed as she hovers over me, one hand on my cock, the other reaching lower to cup my balls.

I feel the friction when it hits my spine. It races through me at breakneck speed. There's no time, so I shout. "Fuck it. I'm coming."

I expect her to pull back, but she doesn't. She hums as the first wave of my release hits the back of her throat and as I hold tight to her head and pump every last drop in, she takes it all.

———

"HOW LONG HAVE YOU BEEN AWAKE?" Linny asks from behind me.

I turn to look at where she's sprawled out on the bed. She's on her back, right where I left her after we fucked.

That happened after I came down her throat.

I was ready to go again almost instantly, the promise of feeling her coming around my cock was too much. I slid on a condom, pulled her on top of me and urged her to ride me until she collapsed after we both came.

After I cleaned myself up and got into bed next to her, she rested her head on my chest.

Her breathing slowed so as she slept, I closed my eyes and imagined a life that included this every single day.

A life where I'd wake up in bed next to her, eat breakfast with her, talk to her about all the bullshit that I can't figure out and then fall asleep in her arms every night.

I can't be falling this fast and this hard for her.

"Not long," I lie.

The truth is that soon dawn will be breaking over Manhattan and I haven't slept a wink. She's drifted in and out all night.

When she rolled over, I got up and moved to the window, looking out at the late summer storm that settled over the city.

"Tell me something about you," she whispers. "Something no one else knows."

That should be easy. There isn't a soul on this earth that knows me well.

I walk back to the bed and sit down next to her.

She's covered with nothing but a thin white blanket. Her hair is a mess and her lips are swollen.

I swear she's more beautiful every time I look at her.

"Something no one else knows?" I repeat back her question.

"Yes." She reaches for my hand. "I want to know one of your secrets."

I slide my fingers over hers, gripping her palm in mine. "I can't swim."

Her lips curve into a smile. "You can't swim?"

I shake my head. "Can you?"

She stretches out on the bed, her legs slipping out from under the blanket. "Very well."

I'm not surprised. It's hard for me to imagine anything she's not good at. "Tell me one of your secrets, angel."

She gazes past me to the window and the rain pelting against it. "Sometimes if I wake up in the middle of the night and it's raining, I go for a walk."

I glance briefly at the window before I look at her. "You do? Why?"

She takes a deep breath. "I was scared of thunderstorms when I was a kid. One night I woke up crying and my dad told me that we'd face my fear together."

Her eyes linger on the window as she talks.

"The storm was passing by the time we got outside, but we walked hand-in-hand for blocks while the rain fell on our umbrellas and the lightning flashed across the sky in the distance."

I listen intently to her while she shifts her gaze from the window to where our hands our joined.

"I was never scared of storms after that night." She slowly rolls onto her side. "There's something hauntingly beautiful about the rain."

"Do you want to go for a walk now?"

Her eyes flicker across my face. "Can I tell you another secret, West?"

I cup her cheek with my hand. "Tell me. Tell me anything."

"I've never made love when it's raining."

I stare at her, my heart stuttering in my chest. "That changes right now, angel."

I slide back under the blanket next to her and tug her close until there's nothing between us but our undeniable raw need for each other.

CHAPTER THIRTY-FIVE

LINNY

IT'S BEEN days since I was with West, but there's still a faint ache between my legs.

I lost track of how many times we made love.

The last time was right before I had to rush from the hotel to my apartment to get ready for work.

West took his time with me, making sure that I came before he chased his release.

I wanted to spend all day in bed with him, but I had a meeting with Ivy and a list of things to do for the Rizon campaign.

We agreed to talk the next day, but missed calls and busy schedules have kept us apart.

This morning a large bouquet of flowers was waiting for me when I arrived at my office.

The small sealed rectangular white envelope held a hand-written card with a simple message.

You in my bed in New York: perfection.

I slid the envelope with my first name on it and the card into the same drawer of my desk where the tiara still is.

I placed the flowers on the corner of my desk, so I could stare at them all day. I did just that until I left my office for this meeting a few minutes ago.

"Good morning, sweetheart."

I look up to see my dad entering the conference room. Mitchell is on his heel with his eyes glued to his phone.

"Hi, dad." I smile. "Did you have a chance to look at the Whispers of Grace website? It's been redesigned and I wanted your …"

"Jeremy just texted me to say they're in the lobby," Mitchell interrupts me.

My dad turns back to him. "Good work, son."

I glance down at my phone. I texted West an hour ago to thank him for the flowers, but I've heard nothing back.

He's an extremely busy man, but I was hoping we could talk briefly before this meeting. I've been anxious about it since my dad arranged it two days ago.

I don't want my relationship with West to impact the job I'm doing. I'm focused and excited about the vanilla vodka launch. I've put a lot of thought and effort into my presentation today. I think it's some of my best work to date.

My head snaps up when I hear Trent's voice approaching. I suck in a deep breath and rise to my feet.

West rounds the corner first, stopping when he reaches the doorway.

He shoots my dad a smile, ignores Mitchell and finally meets my gaze.

"It's good to see you, Jeremy." My dad moves from where he's standing. "You too, Trent."

Both men approach my dad and shake his hand.

Mitchell lines up and does the same.

I don't move. I can't move. My knees have weakened to the point that I fear they'll buckle if I attempt even the smallest of steps.

West is dressed impeccably in a black suit and blue dress shirt and tie.

I'm instantly overwhelmed by an image of what he looks like without a stitch of clothing on.

I need to pull myself together. Now.

"Hey, Linny." Trent raises his hand in my direction. "How are you?"

"Good." I drop back into my seat. "How are you, Trent?"

"Alive." He laughs as he lowers himself into the chair next to me. "I'm finally getting over the flu."

Out of the corner of my eye, I catch West pulling out the chair opposite me.

"That's good news." I pick up my pen. "Your tea should be arriving any minute."

"That's thoughtful, thanks." Trent touches my forearm.

West's gaze follows the path of Trent's fingers, his hand fisting on the table in front of him.

I stretch to reach for my pen, causing Trent's hand to slip from my arm. "I haven't forgotten about the rest of us. I ordered four coffees too."

"Let's get started." West strums his fingers over the edge of the table. "What have you got for me today, Linny?"

I glance over at my dad to find him whispering something to Mitchell. I had him in mind when I envisioned this contest and the attached prize, yet he's more interested in what Mitchell is saying than my presentation.

I tap my pen on the edge of the table. "Gentlemen, you're going to want to hear this."

My dad and Mitchell both turn to look but it's my dad

who chuckles. "The floor is yours, Linny. Once you're done, Mitchell has a fantastic idea of his own to pitch."

I wouldn't be so sure.

Once I'm finished explaining my vision for the Rizon campaign contest, Mitchell's idea won't stand a chance.

I flip to the first page of the notepad in front of me and take a deep breath.

"This is unlike anything you've seen before. I'm calling it a night to remember." I lock eyes with West across the table.

"I just had one of those." His gaze drifts over the neckline of the black dress I'm wearing.

A chorus of male laughter fills the room.

"I wish I could say the same." Trent snickers.

"Me too," Mitchell chimes in as my dad pats him on the shoulder.

I shoot West a look and I'm rewarded with a wicked grin and a lift of his brow.

The man is playing with fire and I'm not going to be the one who gets burned.

I clear my throat to draw the attention back to me. "The winner of the Rizon vanilla vodka launch contest will enjoy a night in Manhattan with a guest of their choosing. They'll experience the best the city has to offer that culminates in their attending the vanilla vodka launch party. I'll see to it that it's a night they'll never forget."

Tipping his chin up, West smiles. "Everyone deserves a night like that."

CHAPTER THIRTY-SIX

JEREMY

HER PEN IS on the move again.

This time she's resting it against the corner of her mouth while we all sample our coffees and add cream and sugar.

David took it upon himself to prepare Linny's coffee for her before he slid it across the table.

I didn't see her as someone who loaded up on the sugar and cream, but judging by the number of sugar packets her dad dumped into her cup, she'll be bouncing off the walls for hours.

I make a note to memory to add just as much sugar and cream to her coffee when I deliver it to her in bed the next time we spend the night together.

She takes a tentative sip. Her brow furrows.

Jesus, she's gorgeous.

"Go ahead, Linny." I snap the lid back on my cup after adding a splash of cream. "I'd love to hear your concept."

Her smile is soft when she looks my way. "Thank you, Jeremy."

My dick hardens instantly at the sound of my name from her lips.

She calls me *West* most of the time. I love that, but this is different. This speaks of a familiarity I want to have with her.

I've always been West to the women I fuck.

I want to be Jeremy to her. I want to be everything to this woman.

I shake that off when she clears her throat again. It's a subtle way of drawing David and Mitchell's attention to her.

It works. They both glance in her direction.

"We've been fortunate enough to work with many wonderful clients over the years." She nudges her eyeglasses up the bridge of her nose. "I took the liberty of contacting several in my quest to create a magical two-night experience in New York City."

I lean my elbows on the table. I wasn't expecting this.

I assumed that the money I was throwing at this campaign would result in attention being lured to my product and my product only.

I'm not sure how I feel about other companies benefitting from this.

"What clients?" Trent asks the question that I was about to.

Linny turns to look at him, her ponytail swaying. "I'll explain."

Trent nods and tosses her a smile and a wink.

The asshole is flirting with her. I should have expected as much given how he couldn't stop talking about how wonderful Linny is on the subway ride here.

"It will be a cross promo between Rizon and the other

clients who have agreed to take part if we get your go ahead." She drops the pen on the table.

"Cross promos can be worthwhile." Trent's hand slides closer to her.

She eyes it and shifts in her seat away from him. "Rizon supplies airfare for two to New York, unless our winner is already here."

I nod. "What else, Linny."

She glances down at the open notepad in front of her. "A two-night stay at the Bishop Hotel in Tribeca and dinner at Nova in Greenwich Village before the launch party."

"Your choices are certainly memorable." Trent breezes his hand over her bare forearm again.

I grip the armrests of the chair I'm sitting in to avoid snapping his wrist in two.

She reaches for her coffee cup, leaving Trent hanging. She takes a long gulp, her eyes pinching shut and her nose crinkling. "I spoke personally to the owners of the Bishop Hotel and Nova. Both were more than happy to agree to supply the guests with Rizon products as part of their experience."

She taps her pen on the notepad. "Mr. Bishop is going to include complimentary cocktails and caviar for the winner in their suite. They'll be served Rizon vanilla vodka, of course."

"I handled the Nova account. Did you consider bringing me in to talk to Tyler Monroe?" Mitchell questions from where he's sitting.

Linny glances over at him. "I dropped in there yesterday and Chef Monroe was gracious enough to join me for lunch. Nova serves Rizon exclusively, so he was happy to agree to a complimentary dinner for two complete with vodka cocktails."

She's covered every base. The fact that she did it without anyone's input is impressive.

"This certainly qualifies as a night to remember," David says.

Linny wags a finger in the air. "There's more."

A smile tugs at my lips. "What else have you planned?"

Her gaze settles on me. "Our winners will also receive two orchestra seats to the New York Philharmonic the night before the launch party. Alexander Donato will be guest conducting the evening they attend."

I'm not a fan of the symphony, so I have no idea if that's impressive but apparently, Trent does.

"You're shitting me," he says with a rub of his shoulder against hers.

Fuck this guy and his touchy-feely bullshit.

Her hand darts to the frame of her eyeglasses. She adjusts them slightly. "I'm serious. A private meet-and-greet with Alexander before the concert will be included too."

"How did you make that happen?" Mitchell drums his fingers on the tabletop. "We've never done any work for the Philharmonic."

She looks over at him, her eyes widening. "I can't reveal all my secrets."

Trent and her dad both laugh. I don't because I see something they can't. I see her determination, her grit. I see a woman who wants the job of CEO and will go above and beyond to get her hands on it.

I see the most remarkable woman I've ever met.

"Each partner in our promotion will be listed as a sponsor on the Rizon website page where we'll feature the contest, its rules and the requirements for entering." She writes something in the notepad in front of her. "My suggestion would be a contest on social media. We can ask entrants to tag the

Rizon official account in a post they make that includes a picture or video of them drinking a glass of Rizon vodka or posing with a bottle."

It's a way to further our social media reach.

"I have our lawyer working on the contest rules as we speak," she goes on. "We'll leave the judging to a panel of Rizon employees. Your pick, of course, Jeremy."

I nod. "It sounds like you've covered all your bases."

She glances down at the notepad in front of her. "I feel a countdown to the launch of the contest will have a tremendous impact. I should mention that Bishop Hotels and Nova have both agreed verbally to prominently feature the contest on their websites. That will link to the Rizon website. I'll get that in writing, but it's a win-win for us. The crossover web traffic will be significant."

I scrub my hand over my forehead. I can't fucking think.

It's a brilliant idea put forth by an incredible woman.

All I want to do is take her in my arms and congratulate her for kicking ass. I want to tell her that I'm proud of her but I can't. Not right now, at least.

She closes the cover of her notepad and places her pen on top of it. "I think that's it. Your turn, Mitchell."

CHAPTER THIRTY-SEVEN

Linny

"GREAT MINDS THINK ALIKE." Mitchell taps one of his fingers on his forehead. "My plan was similar although I was planning on adding a helicopter tour of Manhattan to it and the matinee of a Broadway show."

"That would lessen the impact." West sighs. "Linny's presented a high-end experience that the average tourist wouldn't be able to afford. Helicopter rides and musicals are standard items on the itineraries of most people when they visit New York City."

I couldn't have said it better myself.

I bite back the urge to smile. My presentation went off without a hitch, except for the fact that Trent couldn't keep his hands off of me.

At one point, I thought West was going to crawl across the table and grab him.

"Jeremy and I will discuss your ideas." Trent pushes back from the table. "We're heading back to the office now."

West rises to his feet, buttoning his suit jacket. "Walk us to the elevator, Linny. I have a few questions about the contest for you."

I slide back my chair and pick up my notepad and pen. "I'd be happy to do that."

I'd be happier if I were getting on that elevator with West so we could spend the rest of the day in bed together.

"After you." Trent waves his arm in the air.

I round the table and breeze past West on my way out the door.

I'd call this meeting a success. I'm hopeful that West and Trent see it the very same way.

———

"DO you know how desperate I am to kiss you right now?" West leans against my closed office door.

"You practically threw Trent in the elevator before pushing the button to take him to the ground floor alone." I laugh as I toss my notepad and pen on my desk. "Your desperation is showing, Jeremy."

He tilts his chin toward the floor. "I've heard my name thousands of times from hundreds of different people, but it's never sounded like that before."

"Jeremy?" I repeat it back. "You've never heard it sound like what before?"

He closes the distance between us with a few measured steps. "Like that. I love the way it sounds coming from your lips."

I raise a hand to stop him right before he reaches me. "We can't."

His hands fist at his sides. "I know. I almost pulled the

goddamn fire alarm in the corridor to clear the building so I could get you alone."

"You can have me all to yourself tonight."

He gives a short laugh. "Is that supposed to satisfy me until then? What the hell am I supposed to do with the over-whelming urge I have now to kiss you, angel?"

I take a step closer to him, knowing that I'm tempting fate. "It's supposed to make you think about me all day until that moment when we're alone later and you can kiss any part of my body that you want."

He rakes me from head-to-toe. "I'll kiss every inch of you."

The sound of my office door opening turns West on his heel. I peer past his shoulder.

"Linny." My dad's gaze is cast down to his phone. "Back in the conference room, you mentioned that you wanted to discuss…"

"Dad," I interrupt him. "Jeremy and I were just talking about…"

"Who should judge the Rizon launch contest," West interrupts.

My dad's head pops up. A wide grin sweeps over his mouth. "Jeremy, I was just typing out an email to you, but here you are."

West nods. "What can I do for you, David?"

I catch my dad's expression when he notices the bouquet of flowers on my desk. "I have two tickets to the baseball game tonight. I was wondering if you wanted to join me."

West's shoulders stiffen. "I haven't been to a game in years."

"If you don't enjoy baseball, I'll pass them to Linny and her special someone."

"Her special someone?" West glances at me.

"I believe his name is Roland." My dad approaches the flowers, reaching out to touch one of the delicate petals of a yellow rose. "One of our clients owns a jewelry store. I stopped in there yesterday to pick up a surprise for my wife. I had a good conversation with the owner and her husband. He's the one who let it slip that my daughter was dating a young man. It would have been nice to hear it from her first."

I almost drop to my knees so I can crawl under my desk.

Who knew Jax Walker was a gossip?

"Roland is a lucky man," West says, amusement flashing across his face. "I'm needed back at my office. Thanks for the invite, David, but give those tickets to Linny and Roland. There's nothing quite as romantic as a night at the ballpark."

I rub my forehead.

"I agree with you on that one." My dad shakes West's hand. "We'll be in touch tomorrow."

"I look forward to it." Turning away from my dad, West faces me directly. "Make it a night to remember, Linny."

His play on my words isn't lost on me. "I plan on it, Jeremy."

The arch of his brow and the smile on his lips says it all. I'll be in his arms tonight, right where I belong.

CHAPTER THIRTY-EIGHT

"IF ROLAND IS WITH YOU, he can go straight to hell," West calls out.

I laugh as I toss my purse and overnight bag on a table in the foyer. I just stepped into the same hotel suite that West and I shared a few nights ago.

It's been hours since he walked out of my office. Once he was in the elevator, he sent me a brief text message.

Jeremy: *Make my every dream come true. Meet me at the hotel at 8.*

I waited until my dad left my office before I responded, fearful that the wide grin on my face would give me away.

Linny: *I have a dinner meeting with a client, but I'll be there as soon as I'm done.*

I laughed when his response lit up my phone's screen.

Jeremy: *I'll watch the game on tv while I wait. If I catch you on the kiss cam with Roland, I'm going with Mitchell's pitch, helicopter ride and all.*

"I'm in bed, angel. Come join me."

I kick off my shoes and pad across the floor, rounding the corner to the bedroom with a smile on my face.

It widens when I see West in the bed. He's sitting up with his bare back resting against the headboard. A white sheet is covering his groin.

He pats the bed next to him. "How was your dinner meeting?"

I slip out of the red dress I put on for dinner. The meeting was with a client who circles back to use our services every few years. She owns one of the few bookstores left in Manhattan and every time she comes back to us, we use the same campaign ideas.

Tonight was different. Mitchell suggested a new approach while I listened. It involved an author in residence program and free writing workshops for kids.

Our client was beaming by the time dessert was served.

It was a victory for Mitchell and I conceded on the side-walk outside the restaurant, telling him that I thought he did a great job.

"Leave the bra and panties on." West's hand squeezes his erection through the sheet. "Red is your color, angel."

I slide into bed next to him. "My dinner meeting was fine, but I don't want to talk about that."

His lips brush over mine for a soft kiss. "What do you want to talk about?"

"Roland."

His dark brows pinch together. "Don't say his name when I'm hard as nails."

I reach to run my fingertips over the outline of his cock. "You know that it's over between us, right?"

"I know that you told me you ended it with him. I believe you."

I slide my lips over his chin. "Good."

He reaches to cup my face. "I also know it was hard for you not to correct your dad when he assumed that Roland sent the flowers."

Guilt has been consuming me since that moment. A lie is a lie whether it's direct or an omission. I allowed my dad to believe that Roland sent me that beautiful bouquet. I've kept the secret of my relationship with West hidden from my dad for weeks.

If he finds out that I've been keeping that from him, my future as CEO of Faye & Sons won't be the only loss I'll suffer. My bond with him will be marred as well.

We've always been honest with one another, even when that honesty results in pain.

I slip my hand back into my lap. "Why did you have to pick our agency to help with the vanilla vodka launch?"

His arms circle me, tugging me closer to him. His breath whispers over my cheek. "Blame fate. It led me straight to you. I'll be forever grateful for that."

———

SWEAT MISTS my skin as West drags his body over mine.

"It was so much," I whisper into the still darkness in the room.

"I could eat you for hours." He licks his lips before pressing them to mine for a tender kiss.

I weave my fingers through his hair, relishing in how soft the strands are. "You did."

He lets out a deep laugh and it resonates through me. "It wasn't enough."

I'm sore from his fingers and his mouth, but I want more.

I need more because soon day will break and I'll have to rush home to change before I go to work.

I want to stay, but I know I can't. I know he can't.

"Jeremy," I say his name softly.

"Angel," he whispers back.

I kiss him again, harder this time, tugging his bottom lip between my teeth. "Get a condom."

He groans into my mouth. "Fuck, Linny."

I let out a bubble of laughter. "That's exactly what I want."

He inhales sharply when he pulls back and our eyes meet. "What would it take to convince you to stay here with me?"

I reach up to glide my hand over his cheek. "If you keep looking at me like that, I'll stay."

He presses his lips to mine. "Forever?"

I hear the vulnerability in his voice. I feel it within me too. The unspoken line between casual lovers and more is blurred. It's so blurred that neither of us can see it anymore.

Before I can say anything, he shifts back on his heels and slides to the edge of the bed.

I watch in silence as he opens a condom package and sheaths his cock. His hand runs over the length from root to tip once, and then again.

Spreading my legs, I motion for him to come to me.

He does. He crawls across the tangled bed linens until he's above me again.

Gripping his shaft, I rub him against my cleft. I close my eyes to savor the sensation; that moment right before he plunges into me, and the pleasure takes over.

"Open your eyes, angel." His voice is gravelly, deep and desirous.

I stare into his eyes as he slides his cock into me, each movement almost too much to bear.

We find our rhythm quickly.

He fucks me with slow, even strokes, keeping his eyes pinned on mine.

When he ups the pace and braces his hand on my hip, I moan. It's so deep, so good and when I come around his cock, he buries his face in my neck.

His breathing is ragged and intense when he comes, holding me in place, whispering words against my skin about never wanting to let me go.

CHAPTER THIRTY-NINE

JEREMY

"GET your head in the game, Jeremy." Rocco taps his knuckles on the table. "You're going to walk out of here a poor man."

I don't give a fuck.

I arrived at Rocco's apartment hours ago with a thousand dollars in the pocket of my jeans. I'm down to my last hundred now and it doesn't look promising.

It's rare that I win on poker night, but tonight I've barely glanced at my cards.

Linny Faye has consumed me all day.

I said goodbye to her at the hotel this morning and I haven't been able to stop thinking about her since.

I swear to god I'm falling in love with her.

"I'm out." Dylan Colt, Rocco's friend, drops his cards on the table. "You two can battle this one to the end."

The night started with Rocco, Dylan and me.

Harve showed up an hour later with a case of cheap beer and two hundred dollars.

He lasted five minutes in the game and two beers before he went home to Blythe.

"I almost feel bad for taking your money tonight." Rocco leans back in the wooden chair he's sitting in. "You're clearly not all here, Jeremy."

I laugh. "It's that obvious?"

He places his cards facedown on the table. "Everything alright at home?"

Rocco knows what's waiting for me at my apartment every time I open the door. I confided in him after he showed up there one day unexpected.

"It's not that." I shake my head. "I met someone."

"Someone?" Dylan's dark brows rise. "I've known you for a couple of years and I've never heard you mention a woman."

We're not friends outside these games, but Dylan's a solid guy.

He's drowned his sorrows in a few glasses of vodka during our games and confessed one night that he's been hung up on a woman named Eden for years.

I barely know the guy, but I could see that it tore him up inside.

I took it as a reminder that relationships can destroy a man. I vowed that night, as I often do, that I'd never willingly hand my heart over to a woman.

Then I met Linny Faye.

"I haven't met anyone worth mentioning until now," I fire back at Dylan with a grin. "It's early. We're having fun but Jesus, this woman."

Rocco pushes back from the table and stands. "You deserve it. Enjoy it."

I nod. "I'll take that advice."

"I went over that email you sent with the details of the launch contest for the vanilla vodka," he says as he opens a bottle of beer in his kitchen. "Whoever came up with that is a genius."

"You approve?" I ask with a laugh.

"I'm thinking of hiring them to handle marketing for a few other projects I've invested in. Do you think he'd be open to that?"

I glance back to where he's standing, pride blooming in my chest. I want the best for Linny. I want everyone to know how talented she is. "She'd be open to that. I'll send you her contact details."

He lifts his beer in the air. "I can't wait to talk to her."

I can't either.

With any luck, I'll be next to her within the hour.

———

LINNY: *Why don't you come to my place?*

I glance down at my phone again. I've read her text message at least a half-dozen times since she sent it to me.

It lit up my phone when I was about to leave Rocco's place, penniless and anxious.

I was anxious to see her. The need to hold her had only increased after I told Rocco about her marketing skills. I could talk about the woman all day to anyone who'll listen.

Now, I'm standing on the sidewalk in front of her building.

I called her after I read the message the first time. I asked why she didn't want to meet at the hotel.

In a breathy voice, she told me that she'd prefer to have me in her bed.

It was only after she assured me that Mitchell was on an airplane headed to Boston for a consultation with a client, that I relented.

I won't put her at risk.

The CEO job means everything to her and I'll move heaven and earth if need be to secure it for her.

I type out a quick message after I enter the foyer of the building.

Jeremy: *I'm here. Buzz me up, angel.*
Linny: I'm 502.

I yank open the heavy glass door and make my way to a bank of elevators across the lobby.

I jab my finger into the call button.

I'm about to see Linny in her apartment. I'm about to fuck her in her bed. It feels like we're taking a step forward that we can't retreat from.

Hope isn't a feeling I'm familiar with, but it's there, in my chest, inside my beating heart.

I step onto the elevator, push the button marked five and take a deep breath.

CHAPTER FORTY

LINNY

"DO YOU WANT SOMETHING TO DRINK?" I gesture toward my kitchen. "I have wine and soda. I might have some orange juice."

"Thank you, but I'm good." Shaking his head West takes in the open concept space.

I'm proud of my apartment. I purchased it two years ago. My dad was determined to help me with the down payment, but I politely turned him down.

I wanted my signature on the property documents to mean something.

I did this alone. I earned and saved every penny that has gone into making this one bedroom apartment a home.

"Do you live alone?" He shoves his hands into the front pocket of his jeans.

"Just me and my shoes." I laugh. "I'm not obsessed with nice shoes, but the walk-in closet sold me on the place."

"You own?" His brows perk.

"Every square foot." I wave my hand in the air. "All seven hundred and twenty-two of them."

He looks down at the hardwood floors. "It's a great space and the neighborhood is good. It's a solid investment, Linny."

"Where do you live?"

His hand jumps to his jaw. "Where do I live?"

I nod, narrowing my eyes. "You've never mentioned it. I picture you as a Tribeca kind of guy."

Laughing, he scrubs his hand over the back of his neck. "What exactly does a Tribeca kind of guy look like?"

I rake him from head-to-toe, enjoying the view. He's dressed casually tonight in jeans, a white V-neck sweater and black shoes. He looks sophisticated and sexy.

I'm still wearing the navy blue sheath dress I had on earlier when I met Ivy and Jax for dinner. Ivy wanted to congratulate me on the success of her campaign. I was happy to oblige since it meant dinner at Calvetti's.

"They're hot as fuck and confident. Oh, and fearless." I tilt my head. "And Tribeca kind of guys know how to kiss."

His hands are out of his pockets and on my face before I take my next breath.

"How many Tribeca kind of guys have you kissed, angel?"

I stare into his dark brown eyes. "If you live in Tribeca the total would be one."

A ghost of a grin touches his full lips. "I live on the Upper East Side."

"I'll amend my answer to zero." I perch on my bare tiptoes to press a kiss to the side of his mouth. "Maybe one day I can see where you live."

His answer is lost in our kiss when his lips slide over mine and his hands glide down my back.

———

THE SUN IS FILTERING through the sheer curtains in my bedroom and tossing slivers of light onto West.

He's on his back in my bed with one arm over his head. The other is resting on his stomach.

The sheets are tangled around his legs. The rest of him is bare.

We made love for hours last night, lost in each other.

After his phone rang twice, he turned it off and tossed it onto the cushion of an antique upholstered chair near the window.

I left my phone in the other room, tucked in my purse.

I didn't want there to be any interruptions during our first night together in my apartment.

I rest my head back on my pillow and close my eyes even though I need to get ready for work.

"Angel." His whiskered jaw brushes against my bare shoulder. "Are you awake?"

I open my eyes to the sight of his gorgeous face. There's a faint red mark lingering on his bottom lip from where I bit him last night as he fucked me hard. It was so hard that tears welled in my eyes.

It wasn't from pain, although the sting of him plunging deep only spurred me on more.

It was from pure happiness.

I've never felt this close to a man before. I've never wanted to crawl into someone's arms and stay there.

"Good morning," I whisper, curling my hand under my pillow.

His lips curve into a soft smile. "The best morning."

Running my fingertip over the crimson mark on his lip, I

smile back. "There's evidence here of what we did last night."

His hand sneaks under the blanket to rest between my legs. "Here too. Are you tender?"

I nod silently.

His gaze skims my face. "Was I too rough?"

My fingers caress his bicep. "No. I liked it."

His shoulders tense, the motion flexes the muscle beneath my touch. His hand moves to my side. "There's something, angel. I need to ask you something."

I sense the shift immediately. His jaw tightens and his eyes narrow. A mask of serious contemplation slides over his expression.

"Ask," I say softly. "You can ask me anything."

I've been steeling myself in preparation for him to ask about my past. I know it's coming. The question I've been dreading may drop from his lips in the next ten seconds and I'll answer honestly.

"I know that you ended things with Roland."

I breathe a sigh of relief. *Roland.* He's my immediate past, not my distant and forgotten past.

"I did," I confirm with a nod of my head. "There was never anything between us. It was just two dates."

He glances back over his shoulder. "Forgive me, angel."

"For what?" My heart thrums a beat so loud that I can barely hear my own words.

"For what I'm about to ask you." His voice is quiet and laced with an ache that tugs at my heart.

"Ask, West. Please just ask." I glide my hand up to his neck. "I want you to ask."

"You reached into your nightstand to grab two condoms." He jerks a thumb over his shoulder toward the wooden night-stand that sits next to my bed. "There are a lot of condoms in there. Boxes, Linny. I need to know if you're sleeping with anyone else."

Before I can answer, he's brushing a strand of hair from my forehead. "If I'm out of line, tell me."

"You're not out of line." I swallow hard. "There are a lot of condoms in the drawer."

His gentle smile encourages me. It soothes me.

"There's a card in that drawer too." I gesture over his shoulder. "It's a birthday card."

"A birthday card?" His brow furrows.

Sliding away from him, I rise to my feet. I'm fully aware that I'm completely naked and his eyes are pinned to me, but I round the bed and tug open the drawer.

"I'll find it."

I yank out the box that I opened. Then box after box of unopened condoms, stacking them on top of the nightstand.

"You don't have to do that, angel." West's hand is on my wrist.

I freeze and look down at him. "I do."

I tug my hand free and keep stacking boxes until I see the corner of the bright pink envelope. I grab it and slide it out, handing it to him.

"My friend, Harmony, stayed here with her husband a few months ago when I was out of town." I settle on the bed next to him. "It was a week before my birthday. The morning of my birthday she texted me and told me to open the drawer."

His eyes dart down to the envelope.

I shake my head and bite back a smile. "I opened it and found all the condoms and that card."

"This card?" He waves it in the air.

"Open it."

"You're sure?" he asks with a rise of his brow. "If it's private…"

"It's not." I rest my hand on his bare chest. "I want you to open it."

He does. He slowly slides the card out after a quick glance at my face.

I watch as he scans the front of the card before opening it. As he reads, the smile on his face gives way to laughter.

"Happy Birthday to you and your pussy, Linny. Call it wishful thinking, but here's hoping that this is the year that you both get some action. Love and kisses, Harmony," I recite word-for-word what Harmony wrote in the card.

West hands the card back to me. "I like Harmony."

"I love her." I tuck the card back into the drawer. "I've used two condoms. Just two. Both last night with you."

He reaches for my hand and brings it to his lips, kissing it gently. "I didn't mean to assume anything."

"You were curious." I look over at the boxes of condoms. "I've been curious too. I've wondered if you've been with other women since we reconnected here in New York."

I swallow and continue on, not giving him a chance to say a word. "That day in your office, you said that you hadn't been with anyone since Vegas, but that was in the heat of the moment."

"I meant every single word I said that day, and every day since. There's been no one since we were together in Vegas. I don't want anyone else, angel."

"I don't either," I whisper. "I only want you, Jeremy."

CHAPTER FORTY-ONE

JEREMY

THEY'RE the words I've been craving, even though I didn't realize it.

I wanted that reassurance from her. I needed to hear it from her.

"We'll only see each other," I state, not ask. "You won't sleep with anyone else. I won't either."

She nods slowly. "I'd like that."

I'd fucking love that.

She pushes the condoms back into the drawer. "I should shower."

I should join her, but I've ignored my phone all night. The vanilla vodka is on the precipice of launching and I have a shitload of work to do today.

She starts rising from the bed, but I stop her with a hand on her wrist. "I've never met anyone like you."

A smile spreads across her face. "I've never met anyone like you either, West. Not even close."

"Being here with you last night meant a lot to me."

Her fingers play with the edge of the sheet that's covering me. "To me too. I've never spent the night here with a man before."

It all feels too good to be true.

How in the hell did I find this woman? Twice.

Her fingers move to my chest. "I need to get ready for work."

I do too.

I watch her sexy, lush ass sway as she walks toward the bathroom.

Once the door closes behind her, I'm on my feet searching for my phone.

I know I shut it off in frustration and tossed it toward a chair near the window.

I push my clothes aside and find it, pushing the button to power it back up.

Tugging on my boxer briefs, I'm assaulted with a symphony of noises.

Chimes, bells and dings penetrate the silence in the room.

I scoop the phone into my palm and scan the screen.

Fuck.

I stalk across the room to the bathroom and swing open the door.

She's there, nude and standing in front of the mirror. The shower hasn't been turned on.

"Angel," I say breathlessly, a combination of pure desire for her and fear over what my selfishness last night has cost me. "I need to go."

"Now?" Her brow furrows. "What's wrong?"

My phone starts ringing in my palm. "I have to take this."

"Go." She waves her hand in the air. "We'll talk later."

I turn and shut the door behind me before I put on my

clothes, grab my wallet and keys and race out of her apartment.

———

"I PICKED UP A SANDWICH FOR YOU." Blythe drops a white paper bag on my desk. "I got a call last night."

I look down at my watch. It's well past noon. I made it into the office a half hour ago after spending the morning at the hospital and then at my place. "Thanks for the sandwich."

"You were nowhere to be found." She looks at the chairs opposite my desk. "Can I sit?"

I tilt my chin up. "I won't stop you."

She settles into one, crossing her legs at the knee. The bright orange dress she's wearing is conservative for her. "Can I speak freely?"

Leaning back in my chair, I wave my hand in the air. "Be my guest."

She studies me as if she's choosing her words wisely. "I know that you changed your will."

My jaw tightens. "How the hell do you know that?"

"Your lawyer sent it back over this morning." She sucks in a deep breath. "I opened the envelope to see what it was."

I point to the large white envelope on my desk. "It's clearly stamped personal and confidential, Blythe. Do I need to buy you a goddamn dictionary so you can read up on the definition of those two words?"

A small smile breaks her serious demeanor. "If you do, look up the definition of friend. I consider myself one of yours."

I'd say the same about her, but I'll never admit it.

"I'm worried about you, Jeremy."

I close my eyes to get my emotions in check. "I'm fine.

The update on the will was necessary. I don't plan on dying for the next sixty years at least."

"I'm not worried about that." She shakes her head. "I know why you changed your will. You want to keep your father away from your fortune."

I nod succinctly.

"I know you were with a woman last night." Her voice softens. "I'm worried that you're going to push your happiness aside because you think there's no room in your life for that."

Six months ago I may have felt that, but since meeting Linny, I'm determined to figure this shit out.

I want her. I want the life I already have. I want it all.

"Don't let your father's sins, destroy your future, Jeremy." She moves to stand.

Reaching for the bag she dropped on my desk, I ignore her advice. My father is in my past. That's where he'll stay. "Get back to work, Blythe."

She tosses me a curt nod. "Will do. I'm here if you need me."

CHAPTER FORTY-TWO

I COULD GET USED to this.

I finger the edge of the small white card in my hand. It was delivered with a large coffee that was spiked with too much sugar and cream.

At first, I thought my dad had dropped the coffee on my desk after his afternoon run to the café around the corner, but then I saw the telltale small white envelope with my first name written on it.

It was a perfect match to the two that I'd received before from West.

My breath caught when I slipped the card from the envelope and read the masculine handwriting.

Us in your bed this morning: everything.

It had felt that way; like everything. Everything I'd always wanted in a relationship with a kind and generous man. Everything I'd always wanted in a lover.

Jeremy is becoming everything to me.

"I want those mock-ups on my desk by the end of the day."

I hear my father's voice approaching in the corridor, so I open the bottom drawer of my desk and toss the envelope and note inside.

Guilt wraps itself around my heart.

I can't keep doing this. I can't hide what I feel for West just to advance my chances at the CEO job.

"Linny," my dad happily says my name as he rounds the corner and enters my office. "I got off the phone with Ivy Walker thirty minutes ago."

I wrap my palm around the coffee cup, taking comfort in its warmth.

"I trust she had only good things to say about the Whispers of Grace campaign."

I know that she did. I spoke to her myself this morning and her exuberance carried straight through the phone. I could feel her excitement over the increased interest in her store here in Manhattan and her website.

The next task she's handed me is to create a buzz for her store in Las Vegas.

I've already been jotting down ideas.

"You knocked that one out of the ballpark." He mimes hitting a ball with a bat. "It's not often that we have a client who is that thrilled with the job we've done."

I've done.

I want to correct him, but I don't.

I don't want Mitchell to earn an ounce of credit for this. I'm the one who put in the hours and effort to make Ivy happy.

"She told me about her store in Vegas." He skims his hand over his head. "You'll need to be there for the re-launch."

The pain of what I did in Vegas a lifetime ago still lingers in my father's eyes. I was twenty-one, foolish and naïve.

We never talk about it, but it's always there like an invisible wall between us, keeping us a breath's away from the closeness we shared before I went on that trip.

"I'll handle it," I say briskly. "I've started brainstorming ideas for that campaign."

The corners of his mouth dip into a frown. "I'll take the trip with you. I haven't been west in years."

Trust.

That's what this is about. He doesn't trust me to travel to Vegas and back without a life-changing mistake even though it's been five years since I let him down.

"Am I missing out on a family meeting?" Mitchell appears in the doorway of my office. "What's going on?"

My dad's face brightens as he turns to look over his shoulder. "You haven't missed a thing, son. I was just congratulating Linny on a job well done, and now it's your turn."

I don't have the stomach to listen to my dad applaud Mitchell for his work on the bookstore account.

"I have something pressing I need to tend to." I sigh. "Would it be alright if I caught up with you two later?"

"Of course." My dad stands. "I'm proud of you, sweetheart."

His words ring in my ears as he walks out with Mitchell, closing the door behind him.

I scoop my phone into my palm and text out a message to West.

Linny: *Thank you for the coffee.*

His response is instant.

Jeremy: *My pleasure, angel. I had them make it just the way you like.*

I laugh aloud, realizing that he must have been paying attention to how much sugar and cream my dad dumped into my coffee during our last meeting.

I start typing my response, my pulse quickening.

Linny: *I'd like to cook you dinner at my place tomorrow night.*

I press send and wait.

And wait.

Finally, his response pops up on my phone.

Jeremy: *I'll be there. Name the time and the wine.*

My fingers fly over the screen before I press send.

Linny: *8 and bring a bottle of Rizon vanilla.*

Jeremy: *You're a woman after my own heart.*

He's right. I am. I'm after his heart. I'm falling hard and fast for him. I hope with everything I am that he's falling just as hard for me.

CHAPTER FORTY-THREE

JEREMY

"YOU COOKED THIS, LINNY?" I wave a hand in the air over my empty plate. "You created this incredible dinner in that tiny kitchen of yours?"

Smiling, she points at her kitchen and the pile of dirty dishes littering the counter. "Do you think I ordered take-out and dumped the food in my pots before you got here?"

Yes? No? How the fuck do I know?

I've lived in New York City my entire life. A great kitchen isn't on the top ten list of must-haves on everyone's list when they're looking for an apartment.

Many New Yorkers never cook at home.

I count myself in that group, although the last few years I have eaten more dinners at my dining room table than in a restaurant.

I've never been the one behind the stove though.

"How did you learn how to cook like this?" I take a sip of water.

She eyes me carefully. "On the internet."

I furrow my brow. "You're serious?"

Her head shakes slightly. "I'm joking. I took a cooking class with my friend, Harmony, a few years ago. She wanted to cook gourmet dinners for her fiancé and she didn't want to go to the class alone, so I signed up too and surprised her during the first class."

"You're good friends with her, aren't you?"

She looks down at the faded, torn jeans and short sleeve white sweater she's wearing.

I lost my breath when she opened her apartment door and I caught sight of her. She's barefoot and wearing minimal makeup. Her hair is a mess of curls that are tumbling around her shoulders.

She looks relaxed and content.

I didn't bother changing after work so as soon as I got here, I shrugged out of my suit jacket, lost my tie, shoes and socks. I may not look as casual as she does, but I feel comfortable. I feel at home sitting across from her at her small dining room table.

"We've been friends since we were kids." She sighs. "In high school it was Harmony, Priscilla, Kendra and I. We were inseparable."

"And now?" I ask. "Are you still in touch with the other two? Priscilla and Kendra?"

She forks the last bite of pasta on her plate. "They were with me in Las Vegas. We were there for Kendra's bachelorette party."

"I should send Kendra's fiancé a case of Rizon vodka."

She slides the pasta into her mouth and chews. I watch intently as she swallows slowly. "He's her husband now and why would you send him a case of vodka?"

I lean closer to her. "To thank him for asking Kendra to

marry him. If that hadn't happened, you would never have been on the flight that morning headed to Sin City."

Her tongue slicks her bottom lip. "Who should I thank for you being on that flight?"

I smooth the pad of my thumb over the path her tongue just took. "You can thank me, angel. I had a later flight booked, but decided to get an early start so the night before we met, I called the airline and changed my flight."

Her eyes widen. "Seriously?"

I part her lips with my thumb. "Seriously. I almost missed my chance to see you in that tutu."

Her teeth nip my skin. "Are you always going to remind me about the tutu?"

I pull back and laugh. "Always, angel. I'll never let you forget it."

I want it to be always. I want to remind her a month from now, a year from now. I want to remind her of the day we met forty years from now.

I need to find a way to make that my reality.

———

"CAN you stop by my office the day after tomorrow at three o'clock?" She stretches out on the bed. "I have a surprise for you."

I palm my still hard cock. "The surprise you gave me earlier was more than enough."

She sucked me off after dinner.

She called it dessert. I called it perfection.

After that, we took a bath in her tub with my leg dangling over the side and her fingers strumming over her clit.

She came for me, touching herself as the heat from the

water reddened her skin. Her eyelids fluttered shut the moment she came.

I've never seen anything more erotic.

After that, I carried her to the bed and made love to her.

"I'll be there," I answer as I feather a kiss over the soft skin of her neck. "I take it I need to keep my clothes on for that surprise?"

Her gaze skims my nude body. "If I had my way, you'd never wear clothes again."

"I could arrange that. I wouldn't argue if you locked me in this apartment forever."

Something in her expression shifts. "I think about that. I mean I think about us being together for days on end."

"You're not smiling," I tease.

The corners of her mouth lift slightly. "If only life were that simple. I have a job. You have a company to run. We have families and friends. We can't disappear for days on end."

"I'll take a night here and there for now."

Her fingers trace circles on my bare stomach. "I think about telling my dad about us."

I know it tears her apart inside that she's had to keep our relationship hidden. I see it her face and in her demeanor every time I'm in the same room as her and her father.

"Will you do that after the campaign is over?" I brush a piece of her hair behind her ear. "I can be there when you do that. I'll assure him that you handled yourself with nothing but professionalism when you were working on the vodka launch."

She closes her eyes briefly. "I haven't thought that far ahead. I always get stuck trying to imagine how he'll react to the fact I'm in a relationship."

"I take it he's protective?"

She heaves a sigh. "Overly."

"Has he always been?" I move slightly to lean on my forearm. "Was he one of those dads who interrogated every guy you dated in high school?"

She tugs the blanket up to cover her bare legs. "I didn't date a lot in high school."

"Me either," I confess.

Her brows inch up. "You're kidding? You didn't date in high school?"

I fucked. I didn't date. I didn't see the purpose in putting in the effort to spend time with anyone if I could skip the dinner, movie or hang-out and get right to the fuck.

"I didn't." I gaze up at the ceiling. "I haven't had a serious relationship. I haven't enjoyed spending time with anyone before. That changed when I met you."

Her eyes widen. "West."

I swallow hard, determined to get the words out that have been trapped in my throat all night. "I'm crazy about you, angel. I love being around you. You make me feel things I've never felt before."

The words hang in the air between us as she studies my face, her bottom lip trembling.

I lean closer to her, trailing my finger over her chin. "You don't have to say anything. I just wanted you to know how I feel."

"I love being with you," she whispers. Her hand jumps to the middle of her chest. "I haven't felt this close to anyone in my life, Jeremy. This is all new for me."

"We'll figure it out together." I rest my forehead against hers. "We can do anything together."

Her lips brush over mine in the softest kiss. When she pulls back, she smiles.

This is my world staring back at me. This is my future and I'll do whatever it takes to make this woman mine forever.

CHAPTER FORTY-FOUR

LINNY

HARMONY: *It's not even close to April 1ˢᵗ, Linny. The joke is on you.*

I look down at my phone and laugh at the text message Harmony just sent me.

Her class let out a few minutes ago, so we've been texting back and forth playing catch up.

I just confessed that I've been seeing the man I sat next to on the airplane on our way to Las Vegas.

Linny: *I'll invite him to brunch the next time you come into the city.*

Her response is quick and typical Harmony.

Harmony: *Make it an early dinner and I can be there within the hour.*

I sigh, wishing that I could introduce her to West today. I want him to be a part of my life beyond my apartment and the conference room.

Linny: *I'm actually meeting him (for work) in a few minutes, but I'll introduce you two soon.*

Harmony: *I'll hold you to that. I'm happy for you! Really happy!*

"Linny, let's go," Mitchell calls from my open office door. "Jeremy and Trent will be here any minute."

I grab a notepad and pen from my desk and stand. "Where's my dad?"

He glances down at his watch. "We had lunch with the suits from Vrite Footwear. Dave's still with them."

Dammit.

I'm irritated, but mostly I'm disheartened. I told my dad that I had a surprise presentation for Rizon today. He knew that this was important to me.

"Dave ordered a bottle of the best champagne to toast to my hard work." He raises his arm in the arm and stumbles. "I've never seen him more proud."

I narrow my eyes. "How much champagne did you have?"

Leaning forward, he shrugs both shoulders. "A few glasses."

"I don't need you in the meeting, Mitchell." I round my desk. "Go home and sleep it off."

"No can do, Lincoln." He waves a finger in the air. "Dave sent me to watch the presentation in his place. I have to report back to him."

Disappointment and anger wage war inside of me. This isn't how I envisioned this afternoon, but my issues with Mitchell and my dad need to take a backseat to work.

"You'll sit quietly and listen." I push a strand of hair behind my ear. "Don't mess this up for me."

He doesn't say a word as he follows me out of my office.

———

I RUB my hand over my neck. I've been able to keep my composure around West but today feels different.

Today he's dressed just as he was the first time I saw him on the airplane in the same gray suit and black dress shirt.

The sunglasses he had on that morning were perched on his nose when he entered the conference room.

He slid them off before greeting Mitchell and me.

I glance over at the poster board that's sitting on an easel at the head of the conference table. Right now, a large white sheet is covering it.

It's a last minute addition to the vanilla vodka campaign.

I steal a quick look across the table at West. "Are you ready?"

Trent's gaze jumps up from his phone to settle on my face. He looks to his left at Jeremy. "I'm dying to find out what's under that sheet. Aren't you, boss?"

West nods. "Go ahead, Linny."

I take a deep breath. "As you both know, our aim with this campaign has always been to attract the attention of your loyal customers as well as potential new customers."

West leans back in his chair. "You've done a remarkable job of doing both, Linny. The contest is in full gear. The response has exceeded my expectations."

"Mine too," Trent adds.

I smile. "I hope that you'll see the value in what I'm about to suggest."

Mitchell clears his throat but doesn't say a word. Both West and Trent look in his direction, but I keep my eyes trained on the notes I wrote down before the meeting.

"To further the reach of the Rizon brand, it's essential to create a buzz that can't be ignored." I move to stand. "Getting the Rizon logo and product in front of as many people as possible is our ultimate goal."

West nods. "I can't argue with that."

"Your financial investment in my new idea will be substantial, but you'll be rewarded ten-fold." I finger the edge of the sheet. "I present to you, The Fire Tour by Asher Foster, sponsored by Rizon Vanilla Vodka."

I tug on the edge of the sheet to reveal the poster board. It's a mock-up I had made of a promotional poster that will be used to market Asher Foster's next tour.

The man is a worldwide rock star who is set to launch his North American tour two months from now. The Rizon logo is prominently displayed on the poster, along with a banner at the bottom that states that Rizon is the official vodka of the tour.

"Asher Foster?" West is on his feet. "Is this an idea, Linny, or are we talking negotiations are pending and this is a potential reality?"

I drop the sheet on the floor. "I've spoken to Asher myself. He's on board. He's working out the details with his management team and the touring company, but it's as good as done, provided you can come to an agreement on terms."

West moves toward me but stops himself before he rounds the conference table. "Holy fuck. This is incredible."

Trent stands, his gaze locked on the poster board. "I'm in awe. I don't know what to say."

I feel a rush of pride. I wish my dad were here to see this, but he'll hear about it. Not only from Mitchell, but I'm confident West and Trent will sing my praises to him.

Mitchell clears his throat again, this time rising to his feet. He wobbles in place. "Linny?"

I look over at him. My stomach drops at the sight of the smirk on his face.

He taps his finger against his forehead. "I just remembered something."

Whatever it is, it can't be related to my presentation. "Mitchell, why don't you head to your office? I'll text Hal to get you some coffee."

He waves his hand in the air as if he's swatting my words away. "Didn't you meet your husband at an Asher Foster concert in Las Vegas? That's where you met Corbin, right?"

I stare at him in disbelief. He doesn't know about Corbin. The only person who does is my dad.

"Wait. That's wrong. It wasn't an Asher Foster concert. It was definitely a rock concert though." His words are slow and slurred.

I open my mouth to say something, but I'm at a loss.

"That was the night you eloped, right?" He rubs his bloodshot eyes. "You two hooked up after the concert and then made it official in one of those little wedding chapels on the strip."

My gaze shoots to Jeremy, but his face is impassive. I can't read anything in his expression.

"Mitchell," I manage to get his name out, but can't form another word.

"This is why our dad won't let her go back to Vegas." Mitchell laughs, his hand resting on his stomach. "She loses control if she drinks too much and he has to clean up her mess. You need to keep the vodka as far away from her as you can."

I grip the side of the table for support as I watch Jeremy walk out of the room.

"She loses control if she drinks too much?" Trent looks at Mitchell. "You're as drunk as the day is long, bud."

Mitchell drops back into his chair.

Trent turns to me. "Don't let him bother you. The only

thing Jeremy and I care about is the presentation and you killed that. I'll reach out tomorrow to get all the details."

I look up and into his face.

"You surprised the hell out of us both today." He smiles at me. "You should be proud of yourself."

I don't feel anything but loss. The man I'm falling in love with just walked out of this room and I don't know if I'll ever see him again.

CHAPTER FORTY-FIVE

LINNY

I STARE DOWN at the phone in my shaking hands.

I can't text Jeremy to explain any of this. Calling him doesn't feel right either.

This is a conversation that I need to have with him face-to-face.

I left Mitchell alone in the conference room. I didn't have anything to say to him. He had said it all in front of West.

I drop into my office chair and scroll through the contact list in my phone until I spot his name.

Dad.

The man who promised that he'd never tell a soul that I married a man I didn't know.

He was the only person I called back then when I realized what I'd done. He was on the next plane to Las Vegas with a recommendation from his lawyer for a divorce attorney in Nevada.

He took care of all of the paperwork. He handled every discussion with Corbin Burnell, the man I exchanged vows with.

It was my dad who swore on his life that he wouldn't even tell my mother.

Yet, Mitchell knows.

A knock on my open office door draws my attention back up.

It's a man. He's vaguely familiar to me.

He's tall with broad shoulders, dark hair and blue eyes. He's dressed casually in jeans and a dark blue V-neck sweater.

"Can I help you?" I try to look past him to where my assistant should be, but I don't see anyone.

"You're Lincoln Faye, right?" His hand is outstretched as he approaches me.

It takes every ounce of energy I have to push to my feet. "Yes, I'm Linny."

"Linny," he repeats my name back as he takes my hand. "I'm Rocco Jones. Jeremy Weston and I are business partners. We're friends. He's told me a lot about you."

I study his face, taking in his strong jawline. I saw him at Nova with West. It was the evening I was there having dinner with Roland.

West was so close to me that night and I didn't know it.

Now, it feels like he's a million miles away.

"Jeremy told me about the great job you've done on the Rizon campaign." He studies me. "I'd like to discuss the possibility of us working together."

I should be overjoyed, but work is the last thing on my mind.

"I had a meeting two blocks from here, so I dropped in to

see if you had a few minutes now to talk," he goes on, "I know it's presumptuous, but I thought it was worth a shot."

I rub my forehead. "I'm sorry, Mr. Jones."

"Rocco," he corrects quickly. "It's Rocco."

He tugs his phone out of his pocket when it chimes, scanning the screen. "It's Jeremy."

My heart skips a beat.

"Is he alright?" I ask in a breathless whisper, my voice cracking.

His gaze wanders from his phone to my face. "He needs to see me. He says it's urgent."

I swallow back a sob.

His features soften. "You're her, aren't you?"

A tear streams down my face. "Who?"

"You're the woman he met." The corners of his lips lift into a smile. "You're the woman who put that smile on his face and that hope in his eyes."

I nod. Fear rushes through me that West has lost hope in us since he heard Mitchell talk about my mistake in Vegas.

"I'm going to meet him now." He shoves his phone back into his pocket. "I don't know what he's told you about his life, but Jeremy's a fighter. He's battled some shit that no one should have to and he's always come out on top. If he's as crazy about you as I think he is, whatever is going on between you two isn't going to get in his way."

I should take comfort in his words, but I can't.

I'm the one who didn't tell Jeremy about my past. He should have heard it from me, not from Mitchell.

He slides a business card from the back pocket of his jeans. "Here's my card. Give me a call when you're ready. We'll meet for a coffee and talk shop."

I watch him leave my office, wishing I could follow him, but I can't. I have to give West time with his friend, and I have to face the one man who promised he'd always protect me.

I wipe the tears from my face, pick up my phone and head straight for my dad's office.

Sooner or later he'll show up and I'll be there waiting with all of the questions I need answers to.

CHAPTER FORTY-SIX

JEREMY

I SHOULD BE DROWNING my sorrows in a bottle of Rizon vodka right now, but my palm is cupped around a coffee. I'm at the café around the corner from Linny's office.

I couldn't make it past this point, so I barked at Trent to get back to the office to take my meeting with a supplier, and I landed here.

I reached out to Rocco because he's the only person I know who will help me make sense of this.

He walks through the door with a smile on his face.

For fuck's sake. Why does he have to look so happy when I feel like my world is upside down?

He stalks over to the counter and places an order.

The barista strikes up a conversation with him. I can't hear a word, but her body language says it all.

She wants more than the few dollars he shoved into the coffee mug in front of her marked *tips*.

Rocco's used to the attention. I am too, but the difference

now is that I don't engage women in idol chatter anymore. I don't seek out the *in* that will move things from a casual conversation to a casual fuck.

I haven't given in to the temptation in months because of Linny.

I close my eyes against the urge to call her.

I want answers.

I want her.

Jesus, all I want is her.

"Jeremy."

I open my eyes to see Rocco lowering himself into the seat across from me, two cups of coffee in his hands.

He slides one to me. "The barista made you another on the house. She said you looked like you could use it."

I glance down at the side of the cup and what's written there in blue ink.

Heather.

Followed by a New York based phone number.

I huff out a laugh. "You've got to be fucking kidding me?"

"I just met her." He takes a sip of coffee. "She's beautiful, Jeremy."

"Heather?" I push the cup aside. "I'm not interested."

"Linny." He taps his fingers on the tabletop. "I just came from her office. She's as torn up as you are."

"What the fuck were you doing at her office?" I narrow my eyes.

"I was two blocks over at a meeting and thought I'd drop in to meet the marketing whiz launching our vanilla vodka." He exhales harshly. "She was shaking when I walked into her office."

"So you put two-and-two together?" I question. "Or did

she come out and tell you that we've been seeing each other?"

"Her face gave everything away." He shakes his head. "She looked like someone grabbed her heart and squeezed it until it shattered. When I told her that I had to leave to meet you, I could see the pain."

All the air in my lungs feels like it escapes in an instant. I don't want her in pain. I want to protect her.

"It's none of my business, but I'm here if you want to talk about what happened," he offers.

I called him down here because I need something from him. I don't know if that's advice or just an ear to listen to me.

Either way, I've got to start talking.

"I found out today that she eloped in Las Vegas at some point." I pinch the bridge of my nose to ward off an impending headache. "It surprised the hell out of me."

"That marriage is over?"

"It better be," I shoot back. "I'd never fuck a woman who is attached to someone else. I'd never touch a woman with a husband."

Rocco knows my history. He knows how I feel about cheating.

"She's not the type to fuck around on someone," I say the words easily, confidently. "I'd bet everything I own that the marriage was over as quickly as it happened."

"I'll pass on that bet because I think you're right." He laughs. "You're the best judge of character I know. You can read people. If your gut is telling you that it's over, it's over."

"I feel things for her that I've never felt before." I take a sip of coffee to swallow past the lump in my throat. "I think I'm in love with this woman."

Rocco blinks. "So what the fuck is the problem? Why aren't you telling her this?"

"If hearing her secret shook me to the core, how the hell is she going to react when she hears mine?"

He glances at me. "If she loves you as much as you love her, she'll see those secrets for what they are."

I laugh. "What the hell is that supposed to mean?"

"You've been hiding a part of your life that you should be damn proud of, Jeremy." He picks up his coffee cup. "There's no shame in what happened to you and your reaction to that."

I worked through the shame years ago. Now, it's guilt that I wrestle with.

"I'm proud to be your friend." He leans back in his chair. "Linny will be proud of you too. Talk to her. Give her a chance to prove how much she cares about you."

It's a gamble, but I have to take it.

I don't want Linny finding out about my past the way I found out about hers.

I need to tell her. She has to hear it from me.

CHAPTER FORTY-SEVEN

LINNY

HOURS HAVE PASSED since I got to my dad's office, although it feels like days.

It's past seven p.m. and he's still not here. I finally gave in thirty minutes ago and sent him a text message.

Linny: *I'm at the office. You need to come down here.*

My dad's response was swift considering the fact that he hates texting.

Dad: *I'm dead tired. What's wrong? I'll send Mitchell to take care of it.*

I laughed aloud, the sound vibrating off the walls and out into the empty offices beyond.

Everyone cleared out by six p.m, many of them stopping in the open doorway of my dad's office to ask if I needed anything.

They all looked confused. It's not surprising since they caught me sitting in his chair behind his desk.

I'm still sitting here.

The last message I sent was twenty minutes ago.

Linny: *It's urgent. Only you can handle this.*

It only took a beat until his next message popped up on my screen.

Dad: *I'm on my way.*

I've spent the past few hours rehearsing in my mind what I'll say. That's been punctuated by memories of my childhood.

My dad taught me how to ride a bike in Central Park. He sat in the bleachers of my high school gymnasium cheering Harmony and me on during all those volleyball games.

He watched me graduate from college, and he was the first person I cooked dinner for in my new apartment.

He's always been my best friend and confidante.

I hear the elevator ding its arrival on this floor. He'll walk past my empty, darkened office and then notice the light shining into the corridor from his.

I take a deep breath as his footsteps near.

"I'm here. What is it?" Sweat peppers his forehead, his cheeks flushing. It's obvious that he put in some effort to get here as quickly as he could.

I'm on my feet in an instant. "Thank you for coming, dad."

He clucks his tongue. "You don't look panicked. Is there an actual emergency that warranted me coming down here at night?"

I step closer to him; close enough that he can see the redness of my eyes. "It's an emergency to me."

"You've been crying." He moves quickly toward me. "What happened? Did you lose the Rizon account?"

No. I lost every ounce of trust I had in you, dad.

I glance down at the black sweatpants and college sweat-shirt he's wearing. This is how he looked at night when he used to tuck me into bed when I was a child.

This is the man I miss.

"You told Mitchell about Corbin."

He reaches for something to steady his balance. His shaking hand lands on my forearm. "Linny."

"Why?" It's a simple question, but the expression on his face is anything but that. He looks as though a train is barreling down on him at breakneck speed and there's no time to jump out of its way.

"He said something to you?" he asks somberly. "I made him promise never to mention it."

I laugh unexpectedly. "You made me the same promise."

"I know." His voice is dull, emotionless. He moves away from me seeking out one of the chairs in front of his desk. Lowering himself into it, he glances at me again. "Families shouldn't have secrets."

I take the chair next to him, crossing my legs at the knees. "He's not my family."

His eyes search mine. "He is."

I shake my head vehemently; tired of playing the good daughter who accepts her father's second marriage and every-thing that comes with it.

I stuck around. I stayed when Bethy ran because my dad wanted an heir to take over the family business.

I made nice with Diane and tolerated Mitchell because I could see the joy in my dad when he was around them.

"He is your family. Mom, Bethy and you are mine." I clutch my hands together in my lap.

His eyes well with unshed tears as he stares at me. "Mitchell is your brother."

"Stepbrother, " I spit back. "I don't even consider him that. He's my competition."

His hands fly in the air in a wide arc. "To hell with it. I'm so goddamn tired of the lies. All of the lies."

His words stop me in place. "What lies?"

"He's my son, Linny. I didn't know until he was four-teen." His voice is hoarse. "Diane sought me out when she moved to New York and…"

I stumble out of my chair, swatting his hands away as he tries to reach for me. "No."

"We had a brief affair before I met your mother." He pushes heavily to his feet, following me as I walk across his office to the open doorway. "I never saw Diane again until we met for lunch one day and she told me. We did a paternity test to confirm. I did love your mother, but Diane was different."

My mom.

She had been so brave during their divorce, telling Bethy and me that sometimes people fall out of love. We believed her even though we heard her crying in the bath each night.

This is why.

"You left mom for her?" I turn and face him. "Did you leave mom so you could be with them?"

"Diane didn't want me." He skims a hand over his head. "I wanted to be available in case she did."

Apparently, she eventually changed her mind since they've been happily married for years.

"Why didn't you tell me he's your son?" I point my finger at him. "Why didn't he tell me?"

My dad folds his hands together in front of him. "He doesn't know. I haven't told him. I will. I plan on doing it next year when I hand the reins of …"

A low guttural cry escapes me when I realize the next words he's about to say. I fall to my knees, wrapping my arms around myself. "Oh god. You knew all along that you'd give the company to him, didn't you?"

"My father wanted me to pass it on to my son." His voice quivers. "I'm honoring that request."

I look up at him, grief and disillusionment clouding my view of the man I once thought hung the moon just for me. "I quit."

"No, sweetheart." He scrubs his hand over his face. "You'll stay on. You'll keep doing what you're doing. You'll work with your brother."

"I. Quit." I enunciate both words as I push to my feet. "Effective immediately."

"What will you do? Where will you go?"

I glance down the corridor to my darkened office. "We'll negotiate my severance. I'm taking some clients with me."

"We're family, Linny. Family doesn't abandon family." His shoulders shake. "Let's talk about this tomorrow after we've both had a good night's rest."

"I'm not abandoning anyone. I'm leaving so I can salvage this." I circle my hand in the air between us. "If I stay I'll resent you more. I can't, dad. I have to go."

"I won't accept your resignation." He widens his stance. "I won't."

"Fire me then." I hold my hands over my heart. "I've been in a relationship with Jeremy Weston since we signed the Rizon Vodka contract."

Shock slides over his expression. "What?"

"I'm involved with Jeremy."

"You kept that from me?"

I hold up my hand in the air between us. "Don't go there. You have no right to go there."

He nods in surrender. "How serious is this thing between you two?"

I swallow hard, tears of joy replacing those of sorrow. "I love him."

"You love him?" he repeats back. "How does he feel about you?"

I start toward my office so I can grab my purse and go find West. "I'm about to find out."

CHAPTER FORTY-EIGHT

LINNY

I STAND in the rain in front of the building that houses the Faye & Sons' offices. With thunder rolling over Manhattan, people rush for shelter.

I don't.

It doesn't scare me anymore. I don't need my dad's reassurance that it won't harm me.

I can take care of myself.

I'll find a job with another advertising firm, or I'll start my own.

I'll land on my feet because I have to.

Waving my hand in the air at an approaching taxi, I step back so I won't get splashed as he drives directly into a puddle next to the curb when the car comes to a stop.

I open the back door and slide in. "Central Park West and Seventy-Eighth."

Since I don't know where West lives, I'm heading to the place where I feel closest to him.

It's the hotel where we took a bath together, made love and where I started to fall in love with the man.

As the driver pulls away from the curb, I look up at the building where I've spent so much of my life.

I thought all of my dreams would come true in there.

My dreams have changed. I've changed and what I want most can't be found in an office or behind a desk.

I want a life with Jeremy.

I hope he wants the same with me.

———

I BREATHE a sigh of relief when the green light flashes after I swipe my key card.

On the elevator on my way up to this floor, I had a brief moment of panic, wondering if West had given up the room.

I push open the door and walk into the darkened suite.

Tossing my purse onto a table in the foyer, I kick off my shoes.

My dress is next. I slide it down my body before I step out of it. It's wet from the rain, so I scoop it up and fold it over the back of a chair in the main living area.

I stand in the silence shivering. I close my eyes, willing my phone to ring so I can hear Jeremy's voice.

I haven't reached out to him since he walked out of the conference room earlier.

I don't know where his head is. I don't know what I'll say to him.

"Angel."

Tears prick the corners of my eyes when I hear his voice. I turn quickly.

He's there, standing in the shadow of the bedroom door.

"Angel," he repeats, his voice thick with emotion. "You're here."

His hair is a tousled mess; he's barefoot and shirtless. The button and fly on his pants are undone.

He looks just as he does when he's about to fuck me.

Is that what I've walked in on? Is there someone else here?

My stomach rolls, my hand jumps to my mouth. "I'm sorry. I'll go."

"What the fuck?" He's on me before I can reach my dress. "Why are you leaving?"

He scoops me into his arms, pulling my back into his bare chest.

All of the emotions of the day hit me full force and my knees buckle as he clings to me. "I hoped you'd be here. I thought it was our place. I'll leave you alone with her."

My words tumble together in a sobbing mess.

He presses his lips to my head. "Angel, stop. Please, baby, just stop. I'm here. It's just me. This is our place."

"I... I thought..."

"I know what you thought," he interrupts me with a kiss to my forehead. "You're dead wrong. I can't fuck anyone else, angel. I won't. I love you. It's only you."

I almost collapse from the words. *Those words.*

"I love you, Jeremy."

He spins me around in his arms until I'm facing him. I see the same sorrow in his eyes that I've felt since he walked out of my office.

"Say it to my face." He cups his strong hands over my cheeks. "Look me in the eye and say it."

"I love you, Jeremy Weston," I say softly. "I really, really love you."

"I love you too." His lips brush against mine. "I was just

about to take a shower. We'll do it together. I'll wash you. I'll take care of you."

I nod. "I need to explain. I want to tell you about Corbin."

The pad of his thumb runs over my bottom lip. "You will. You'll tell me about him."

"I didn't love him." I press my lips to his. "I've never been in love before."

He pulls back to look at me. "I've never been either. I don't know how to do this, angel, and there are things… things I have to tell you."

My heart races with that confession. "They won't change how much I love you."

"I pray that is true." His voice is hoarse.

I stare into his dark eyes. I see the pain that's always swimming there. "Let me help you with your burdens, Jeremy. I'm strong enough to carry them with you."

He moves swiftly, scooping me up into his arms like I'm a bride. "Let's wash today away in the shower and then we'll talk. It's time."

It is time. It's time for all of our secrets to be revealed.

CHAPTER FORTY-NINE

JEREMY

"TELL ME ABOUT CORBIN."

It might be buying time, but I want to know about him. I've been waiting all day to hear about the man who she said '*I do*' to in Vegas.

She leans back on the couch, the fluffy white robe she's wearing opening to reveal her lean legs.

I wrapped it around her body after we showered.

Washing her was arousing. I wanted to drop to my knees and taste her. I yearned for her touch on my cock, but I needed the tenderness more. She did too.

I took care of her while the warm water pelted down on us.

We didn't speak. There was no need for words.

Now, that we're dried off and sitting across from one another, words are all we both crave.

"There's not a lot to tell." She tucks her legs beneath her.

"We met in Vegas. I was twenty-one. He was a year older than me."

My foot taps on the floor as I listen.

I pulled on boxer briefs after our shower. That's all I'm wearing now as I sit in a chair.

"I went there to treat myself." She looks toward the window. "I took the trip with a bunch of girls I'd met in college. I wasn't close to any of them, but when they said they were going to Las Vegas for a concert and they had an extra ticket, I jumped at the chance."

"Vegas can be hard to resist." I smile.

"Yes." Her eyes meet mine. "I was a virgin."

That stops my heart for a full beat. "You were a virgin?"

"Twenty-one and never been touched." She manages a small laugh. "I had been touched, but my experience was very limited."

I'm not going to ask why she was still a virgin. I know why. She's protective of herself. I could tell when she showed up at my hotel suite in Vegas that it wasn't something she'd done before.

"I mentioned it to one of the girls on the trip and it took all of two minutes until everyone knew." Her eyes close briefly. "I was embarrassed. I thought something was wrong with me."

Jesus. I wish I would have known her then. I wish I could have been there to tell her that she was beautiful and desirable.

"There was nothing wrong with you," I say softly.

Her gaze drifts to my face. "I know that now. I do, but back then it felt like I needed to change it as soon as possible."

"So you slept with Corbin?"

Her head shakes. "We never did. I never saw him without his clothes on."

I raise a brow. "I'm not following. Mitchell said you hooked up with Corbin and then got married."

"Mitchell was wrong." She looks down. "Corbin was a virgin too. He promised his parents he'd wait until he was married, so after a few drinks, we both thought marriage was a good option."

I smile. They were just two innocents with an attraction to each other and a skewed view of what was right.

"We went to the chapel," she goes on with a faint smile on her lips, "I wore jeans and a tank top. Corbin wore jeans and a T-shirt and an Elvis impersonator pronounced us husband and wife."

"And then?" I question with a roll of my hand in the air.

She sighs. "We went back to the hotel room he was sharing with his friends. He kicked them out, went into the bathroom and got sick. By the time he crawled into bed with all of his clothes on, I was sobering up. I called my dad. He freaked out and caught the next flight to Vegas."

"It was annulled?"

Her eyes skim my face. "It was. My dad took care of everything. I never spoke to Corbin again."

"Your dad is a good man." I rub my forehead. "He's always there for you, isn't he?"

Her bottom lip quivers. "Something happened tonight."

I move quickly, rounding the coffee table between us until I'm next to her. I wrap my arm around her, tugging her into my chest. "Tell me, angel. What happened?"

She looks up at me, her vivid green eyes unreadable. "I quit my job."

"Because of what Mitchell did in the conference room?" I

tilt her chin up with my finger. "He was drunk, Linny. It doesn't change anything about your work on our account."

Her eyelids flutter shut. "No, it's not because of that."

I whisper a kiss against her forehead. "What then?"

Her eyes lock on mine. "Tonight, my dad told me that Mitchell is his biological son. He'll be taking over the company next year once my dad retires."

What the actual fuck?

"Mitchell is your brother?" The question sounds ridiculous, even though it seems to be grounded in fact. "Your dad is handing him the company."

"He said that my grandfather wanted it to be passed on to my dad's son." She rests her head against my chest. "That means it's going to Mitchell."

This woman gave her all to her job. She has talent beyond measure and her father is going to ignore all of that to hand the reins of his company over to his incompetent son just because he has a dick?

"I'm sorry, baby." I tug her closer. "Jesus, you've been through so much today."

She takes a deep breath. "The hardest part of this is I don't know what to feel for my dad anymore. He's not who I thought he was."

"I can help with that," I whisper.

"You can?" She shifts in place to look up at me. "You've never talked about your parents. Did your dad let you down too?"

This is it.

This is when I tell this beautiful woman everything.

"We let each other down." I stop and think about the next words I'll say. "My father is in prison because of me."

CHAPTER FIFTY

LINNY

PRISON.

That's beyond the scope of what I imagined whenever I pictured Jeremy's family.

There was nothing online about his parents.

The only familial connection I've been able to make is that he inherited Rizon from his mom's father.

I got that from the Rizon website. It was written in a short paragraph about how the company was founded and its history since then.

I ask the obvious question because I don't know what else there is to say. "What did he do?"

"He fucked up the lives of his children," he says, his head bowed. "He ran an investment firm. He stole from every one of his clients. From me too."

I'm speechless.

Hours ago I thought my dad had hurt me in an inconceivable way, but his failings were based on his selfish need to give his son the world.

From what Jeremy's saying, his father's actions were purely selfish.

"I interned for the firm that he ran with his third wife." His head falls back onto the couch. "I saw things that didn't add up. None of it made sense. I didn't know what to do."

"How old were you?"

He tilts his head to look at me. "Nineteen, twenty. Old enough to know that something wasn't right."

I reach for his hand, cradling it between my own. I need him to feel reassured, to feel my presence in every way.

"I was in college, and it happened over two summers." He circles my hand with his thumb. "The first year I thought it was an accounting error. I mentioned it to my dad, but he said it was nothing. He called it an oversight and told me to forget about it."

"Did you?" I ask warily.

"No." His jaw tightens. "It bothered me. It ate at me. I went back the next summer and the first thing I did was pull up that account on my computer. The numbers still didn't add up."

He shifts slightly, his legs parting. I can feel the tension knotting his body.

"I pulled up another account; my account." His eyes close. "I had inherited a trust when I was eighteen from my mother's family and Rizon when I was twenty-one. I was the only child; the only grandchild."

"Your father invested the money in the trust for you?"

"I didn't think twice asking him to handle that for me." He huffs out a pained laugh. "If you can't trust your father, who the fuck can you trust?"

I'm not the person to answer that.

"Was it all gone?" I squeeze his hand in mine.

His gaze skims my face. "I couldn't access it, so I asked him about it. He gave me some bullshit excuse about keeping it under lock and key because of the other employees. He promised he'd get me a printout of it, but that never came."

It's a betrayal that's about so much more than money.

He moves to stand.

"He gave me his assistant's password to login to the system." His hands rake his hair. "That's why I had access to everything. The more I searched accounts, the more discrepancies I found."

"Did you bring it up to your dad?"

"Hell no." He turns back toward me. "I listened to him lie on the phone to clients. They'd call wanting to cash out an investment and he'd tell them the timing was off, or he'd need a couple of weeks to pull the paperwork to release it."

His hand lands on his bare stomach. "He'd take money from someone else's account to pay out the first. It was a circle that was collapsing on itself."

I slide to my feet. "What did you do?"

He takes a deep breath. "I turned him in. I went to the police, they got the feds involved, and I gave them all the evidence they needed to put Craig Weston and his wife away for the rest of their lives."

_____

I STAND BEHIND him watching him.

He's been staring out the window for the last ten minutes since he told me that he turned his father in.

He's a brave man.

"You did the right thing, Jeremy."

He looks at my reflection in the glass. "Not everyone would agree with you."

I move closer to him with unsteady steps. "I'm sure your father and his wife wouldn't agree, but they're criminals."

He turns to face me. "They are."

I tug on the sash of the robe to tighten it. "I'm glad you told me."

"There's more."

I freeze.

"That's not even the part that matters, angel." He glances up that ceiling. "Jesus, I wish that was all I had to tell you, but you're going to need to sit back down for the rest of it."

I stay standing. "What else is there?"

His phone starts ringing in the distance. He looks toward the bedroom, but he doesn't move from where he's standing.

"Do you need to get that?" I ask quietly. "I can wait here if you need to get it."

"I love you, Linny." His voice cracks. "I need you to know that."

Tears well in the corners of my eyes, fear squeezing me from the inside out. "Please tell me what it is. What are you keeping from me, Jeremy?"

His phone stops ringing, only to start again a few seconds later.

"I'll show you." He holds out his hand to me. "Get dressed and I'll show you."

CHAPTER FIFTY-ONE

LINNY

HE'S BEEN silent since we left the hotel.

We both dressed quickly. He wrapped his suit jacket around my shoulders after I put my dress back on.

I thanked him.

He told me he loved me again.

I didn't say it back. I couldn't. I felt it within every cell of my body, but until I know what's waiting for me at the end of this taxi ride, I can't form the words.

We're headed to the Upper East Side.

He gave the driver an address on East Sixty-Third Street.

I'm not familiar with that part of Manhattan. I don't know if we're going to his home or another hotel.

I don't know anything other than how much I care for this man.

"This is it," he says hoarsely to the driver as we pull up in front of a townhouse.

He slides some money from his wallet and hands it to the driver as I peer out the window.

This has to be where he lives. It's a beautiful brick building.

I wait while he exits the car. He holds his hand out to help me get out. I take it, welcoming his touch.

"Do you live here?" I ask tentatively, not wanting to assume anything.

He nods. "My grandparents lived here. They left it to me."

It's not just rich in the history of the city. The memories it holds for him makes it priceless.

"It's a huge place just for you," I say teasingly, wanting to lessen the anxiety I'm feeling.

He brings my hand to his lips, kissing it softly. "I don't live alone, angel."

As the words leave his lips, the front door swings open.

We both turn to look at the sight of a teenager dressed in torn jeans and a dark hoodie standing just inside the foyer. The light from within illuminates his face.

His hair is blonde and curly.

He waves his hand in the air toward us, as he shouts, "Germany is home."

A young woman wearing a blue T-shirt and yoga pants appears in the doorway too. She's breathtaking. She must be in her late teens or early twenties. Her golden brown hair is falling around her shoulders in soft waves.

"Hey, Jer." She smiles at us both. "Is that her? Did you finally bring Linny to meet us?"

"This is her." Jeremy wraps his arm around my waist. "Linny, I want you to meet Breccan and Athena, my brother and sister."

―――――

JEREMY CLOSES the door behind us as we step into the foyer.

"I'm Zachariah." A boy with a cast on his left arm approaches us. He looks like he's twelve or thirteen-years-old. "It's a family name. I don't like it."

"My name is Lincoln, so I feel your pain."

He laughs. "Lincoln? As in Abraham Lincoln?"

I shrug. "It was my grandfather's name."

"Mine was the name of my mom's brother." He rolls his blue eyes. "I never met him, but I think he must have been a pretty cool guy."

My gaze slides over the light blue skate shorts and white hoodie he has on. They compliment his olive skin and black hair perfectly.

I point at the cast on his arm. "What happened there?"

He looks down at it. "Skateboarding."

"He sucks." Breccan laughs. "Like totally sucks. We spent hours in the hospital waiting for him to get patched up because he took a spill."

"Shut up." Zachariah waves his casted arm in the air. "Like you could do better."

"Any day of the week." Breccan leans his hip against the wall.

"Do you know anything about seventh-grade algebra?" Zachariah turns his attention back to me, wiping his hand under his nose. "Germany doesn't and he's no help with my homework."

I giggle. "Germany?"

"He had the flu a couple of years ago." Breccan grabs his stomach in jest. "He kept telling us to stay out of his room because of the germs. We've called him Germany since."

I scan the faces of Jeremy's three siblings. They don't resemble one another, or him.

Jeremy looks down at his watch. "It's getting late, Zach. You should get to bed."

"It's Friday night."

"Shit. Today was a bitch. I lost track of what day it is." Jeremy laughs.

Zachariah shakes his head. "And he tells me not to cuss."

"That's a privilege reserved for age." Jeremy pats him on the shoulder. "Linny and I are going to head down the block to the pub for a drink before I take her home."

"We cook spaghetti every Sunday and watch a movie. Do you want to come?" Breccan jerks his thumb over his shoulder toward what looks like the main living area.

We haven't made it past the foyer.

"Our spaghetti is the ultimate," Zach chimes in. "Say you'll come."

I look over at Jeremy. His eyes are filling with tears.

"I'll be here." I nod my head. "I wouldn't miss it for the world."

CHAPTER FIFTY-TWO

JEREMY

FEAR CAN BRING a man to his knees. It can stop him in its tracks.

That's what mine did to me. My fear of telling Linny about my father and my fear of what she'd feel knowing that I've taken on the task of caring for Athena, Breccan and Zach.

She walked into my townhouse filled with grace and compassion, even though I sent her in there blind.

She hasn't said much since we sat down at a table in this pub. It's a stone's throw from my front door.

I come here when I need a minute to breathe or think. The bartender knows me by name and by drink.

I surprised her tonight when I ordered two glasses of soda.

Linny didn't want anything stronger. I didn't either.

I feel like I'm emerging from a haze and I don't want anything to impact the clarity I'm finally feeling.

"Why didn't you tell me about them?" She sips from her glass. "They seem wonderful."

"They're incredible." I smile with pride. "Zach is at the top of his class. The kid is a fucking genius. Athena is majoring in business at NYU and Breccan is the star quarterback at his high school. He's going to land a full scholarship. I know he will."

She smiles softly. "Did you think I would be less interested in you because of them?"

I reach for her hand. "I've never done this, Linny. I've never told a woman about them. Only a handful of people in my life know about them."

"You're protective of them."

It's a statement of fact, not a question. She's right. I am.

"They haven't had it easy," I explain. "They were raised by their mom, Simone Millett. She did the best she could, but she struggled financially until she met my dad."

"What about their dad?"

"Dads." I correct her.

Her hand squeezes mine. "Do you all have different fathers?"

I nod. "They don't know their fathers. They have no other family. Simone struck a plea deal with prosecutors but it still meant years of prison time. The kids were going to be sent to foster care. I couldn't let that happen."

She bites her bottom lip. "You took them in?"

"I had to." I tap my fingers over my chest. "They would have been separated."

"That's an incredibly generous thing to do." Her gaze scans my face. "Most people wouldn't do that."

"I wanted them to have stability." I look up when a couple walks into the pub. "I needed them to know that they could count on someone to always be there for them. I had to be that person for them."

"They seem very happy." Her face brightens with a smile. "You're a family. I could see that right away."

I huff out a laugh. "It wasn't always that way. The boys hated me at first because I'd turned their mother in. Athena was different. She understood, but Breccan and Zach didn't forgive me for a long time."

"That had to have been rough."

I take a sip of soda to swallow past the lump in my throat. "It was hell. I had to get my cousin, Cindy, to step in to help. She moved in with us for almost a year. She still helps out. She stops by my place every day so she can be there when the boys get home from school. They're old enough to fend for themselves, but I never want them to feel alone."

"Cindy was with you at the Nova party." Her brows lift.

"I wanted her to have a night out," I tell her. "It meant a lot to her to be there."

"You surprised me tonight." She pulls my hand up to her face and feathers a kiss over my palm. "I knew you were special, Jeremy, but it's more than that. You're a hero."

"I'm not a hero." I lean in to kiss her softly. "I'm a guy who is trying to get through this life one day at a fucking time."

The corners of her eyes well with tears. "Everything changed today."

"You've been through hell." I wipe a tear from her cheek as it falls. "Let me take you home and get you into bed."

"You can't stay with me tonight, can you?"

I kiss her again, harder this time. "I want to, but I know that three people are waiting for me at my place with a million questions about the woman I love."

"Tell them only good things about me, okay?"

I laugh. "I'll tell them that you're my angel."

"What time is spaghetti dinner on Sunday?" She asks with a grin.

"I'll pick you up at four." I brush my fingers over her cheek. "What are you doing tomorrow?"

"Figuring out the rest of my life." She sighs. "I'm going to clear out my office and decide what my next step should be."

"The Rizon account is yours." I kiss her temple. "I have no problem breaking the contract with Faye & Sons."

"My dad will let me take your account." She stares into my eyes. 'I think I'll start my own firm. I know it will take time to build up a client base, but I have some savings and a lot of connections."

"I'll be there every step of the way if you need me, Linny."

"I'm here for you too." Her hand brushes my chin. "I'll always be here for you."

CHAPTER FIFTY-THREE

LINNY

"YOU WEREN'T KIDDING." I wave my fork in the air toward Zach. "This is awesome spaghetti."

"I know, right?" He spins his fork on his plate, picking up another long noodle. "If we all work together, it turns out just right."

That's exactly what they did.

I sat by the large granite island in the massive kitchen, while Jeremy and his siblings worked side-by-side to create a meal of homemade meat sauce and pasta, garlic bread and a side salad.

They teased each other while they maneuvered around the kitchen, each with a specific job.

"Sorry again about the wine," Jeremy apologizes for a second time.

It's what I asked for when he offered me a drink after we got here. He was quick to explain that he doesn't keep any alcohol in the house.

It's admirable.

I settled on an iced tea with lemon.

"How did you meet Germany?" Breccan asks from where he's sitting opposite me at the dining room table.

The brownstone is large, covering three floors.

I was given a tour by Athena right before dinner was served.

The main floor is home to the kitchen, the formal dining room, a library, a living room and a bathroom.

We went up one flight of stairs to three bedrooms, each with their own bathroom, and then another flight to where the master suite is.

The entire townhouse is decorated in a contemporary style that compliments the dark hardwood floors and antique light fixtures.

It's a home. A warm home filled with love.

"Do you remember when I went to Las Vegas a few months ago?" Jeremy takes a sip of water. "I met Linny on the flight there. She was wearing a pink tutu and a tiara."

A chorus of laughter fills the room.

"A tutu and a tiara?" Athena's thickly lashed blue eyes widen. "Do tell, Linny. What was that about?"

I place my fork on my plate. "I was going there for a bachelorette party. I was a bridesmaid. There were three of us on the airplane dressed like that."

Breccan looks down at a spot of meat sauce that has settled in the center of his white T-shirt." Jeremy's eyes must have bugged out of his head."

I laugh as I glance to my left to see a smile on Jeremy's face. "I looked ridiculous."

"You were beautiful," he says with a chuckle. "I saw Linny again when I hired her father's advertising firm to help with the launch of the vanilla vodka."

"Fate put you together twice?" Athena brushes her hand over her bare shoulder. She's wearing a pink off-the-shoulder sweater and dark jeans.

They're all dressed casually, including Jeremy who is wearing jeans and a football jersey.

I tried on three outfits at my place before I decided on a denim dress and black ankle boots.

"It was meant to be." Jeremy winks at me. "I'm grateful every day that I met her."

"Do you love her?" Zach looks at Jeremy.

"Zach." Breccan's voice comes out with a snap. "You don't ask people that."

"Very much," Jeremy answers. "I think it was love at first sight for me."

"Was it for you too, Linny?" Zach looks across the table at me. "Did you love him the first time you saw him?"

"I felt something I've never felt before." I reach for Jeremy's hand under the table. "He made me feel safe. Love grew pretty fast from there."

"Can we eat the chocolate cake that Linny brought for dessert now?" Zach moves to stand. "I'll clear the plates."

"Let's load the dishes into the dishwasher and then we'll pick a movie and have dessert." West is on his feet too.

As they leave the room, followed by Breccan, Athena moves to sit next to me.

"He needed you," she says in barely more than a whisper. "He's given everything to us for years."

"I needed him too." I smile at her.

She circles her finger on the linen tablecloth. "Take really good care of his heart, Linny. It's been through a lot."

I nod. "I promise I will."

"I'm glad he found you." She rests her hand on mine.

"My brother saved us. He showed us that it was okay to be happy again. We want him to be happy now."

"I want that for him too, Athena."

"When he told us about you, he said you were an angel." She gently squeezes my hand. "He was right."

The sound of glass shattering pulls her to her feet.

"Zach isn't great with one hand." She laughs. "I'm going to go help. I'm glad you're here."

"Me too," I say, trying to level the emotion in my voice. "There's no other place I'd rather be."

CHAPTER FIFTY-FOUR

JEREMY

"ARE you going to invite me in?" I ask with a grin. "I've been on my best behavior all night, but my cock can't take anymore."

She glances down at the front of my jeans. "You're hard."

"I was hard in the taxi when you kissed me. " I lean forward to kiss her. "The way you ran your tongue along my bottom lip, made me think about how that would feel over the head of my dick."

Her cheeks flush. "You have time to come up?"

"I can stay the night." I pocket my phone. "Athena doesn't have class tomorrow so she'll be there when Zach wakes up. She'll get him off to school."

"Tonight meant a lot to me." She looks down the street when a car horn blares. "I felt like I belonged there."

"You belong there," I stress the words. "They want you back next Sunday, angel."

She did belong there. She sat next to me as we watched a comedy with my siblings. She was quick to toss popcorn back at Zach when he leveled a handful at her.

I saw the look on her face when Athena hugged her good-bye, followed by Zach. Breccan gave her a fist bump, which for him is akin to a full-on embrace.

In my wildest dreams, I couldn't have imagined a scenario where the love of my life fit into my family with such ease.

"I'll be there." She fishes in her bag for her keys. "I want them to like me, West."

"They do." I take the keys from her hand and motion toward the doors of her building. "I know you just met them, but I'm telling you, Linny, they're hesitant when it comes to meeting new people. Trust is about as easy for the three of them as it is for me."

She yanks on my hand to stop me. "I would never hurt them, or you."

"I know." I kiss her palm. "We're going to take this at the pace that works for all of us. We'll stumble and make mistakes. Things will get messed up because that's how it works with them and me, but we keep moving forward. You're part of that now."

I see the hesitation in her expression, so I keep talking to soothe that anxiety. "I know it's a lot, Linny. I'm not asking for anything more than what you can give."

She stares at me. "My life is upside down right now."

I pull open the main door of her building and follow her through. "Did you clean out your office yesterday?"

She stops in the lobby and turns to me. "My dad was there. We talked briefly. He's going to give me some time and space."

"That's good."

"I'll be taking over your account and one other that means a lot to me. " She rubs the back of her neck. "It's a jewelry store. Whispers of Grace."

"Ivy Walker's store?" I ask with a smile. "Jax's wife?"

Her head tilts. "You know them?"

"Jax is an old friend." I reach to touch her shoulder. "I was going to ask if you wanted to be my date to his surprise birthday party next week."

"You mean non-surprise party." She rolls her eyes. "He knows all about it. I was invited too."

"We'll go together." I squeeze her bicep. "It will be our first official event as a couple."

"The vanilla vodka launch party will be our second."

I point to the elevator. "The second of many, angel. I need to fuck you so get your ass on that elevator."

The lures a smile to her perfect lips. "You know just what to say to me."

I lean down and whisper in her ear, "I know just what to do to you too."

———

I GLIDE a hand under her bare ass and tilt her body to just the right angle so I can slide my cock against her tender core.

"You're teasing me." She slaps a hand over my shoulder. "Enough, Jeremy. It's been so much already."

She's wrong. It's not been enough.

I ate her sweet pussy the second she closed her apartment door. I was on my knees with her dress bunched at her waist, and her panties a torn mess on the floor.

She came against my mouth twice before I took her over my shoulder and carried her to her bed.

I stripped us both and kissed her deeply while I fingered her to another orgasm.

I'm on top of her now. My cock is sheathed and aching.

I'm harder than I've ever been because she whispered the words that I'll never get enough of.

"I love you."

They fell from her lips as she came the first time.

"Fuck me, West."

My cock jumps. "Say it again, angel."

She moves until her lips are barely touching mine. "Fuck me."

I drive into her, pushing her up the bed.

"Ah, yes." She moans. "Like that."

I move slowly, squeezing her ass with each pump. "Like that, baby."

"Why is it always this good?" Her eyes find mine. "Why does it feel like this every time?"

The need to fuck is consuming. I up the pace, thrusting harder and deeper. "It's love."

"Love." Her voice is so soft that it's barely audible.

Her eyelids flutter shut, her lips part and she moans over and over as I drive my dick into her beautiful body.

Tears well in my eyes at the sight of her coming.

The pure pleasure in her face and the tightening of her body around mine as she comes is almost too much.

I fuck her hard as I chase my own release.

I slam into her over and over again, wanting her to feel more, needing her to come again.

She does with a loud cry and it sends an orgasm crashing through me.

"I love you, Jeremy," she whispers as she clings to me.

"Angel, I love you with everything that I am."

"With everything that I am," she repeats back with a tender kiss to my neck.

I wrap my arms around her, holding her against me.

"I need to sleep." She rests her head on my chest. "In your arms is the only place I want to be."

It's the only place I want her to be, tonight and forever.

EPILOGUE

1 YEAR LATER

Linny

"I THINK our spaghetti gets better every week." I push my plate back. "I ate it all."

Zach looks over at where I'm sitting. "I still ate more than you, Linz."

He's grown at least four inches since I met him a year ago and his voice has deepened. He's not a child anymore. He's a young man with his sights set on becoming a doctor.

I know he'll do it.

I look at Jeremy. He's sitting next to me. He's nervous. His bare foot is tapping on the floor. I reach over and squeeze his hand to soothe him.

"Give me a few more months and I'll eat more than all of you combined." I chuckle.

Athena's head pops up. Breccans's too.

"What is that supposed to mean?" Zach fires back. "You've been living here for six months now, and you eat less than any of us."

"I can't include Athena in that," he goes on, pointing at his sister. "She's at school most of the time."

She is. She'll graduate in just a year with a business degree and a bonus certificate. She's been spending her evenings and Saturdays studying floral design.

Jeremy and Rocco are both eager to invest in her first venture. She's going to open a flower shop that serves specialty coffee and tea. She'll offer floral design courses as well.

My firm, Lincoln Dawn Communications, will handle the marketing.

I've spent the past year building my business from an office in Chelsea with Hal as my second-in-command. I had a boost after the Rizon vanilla vodka launch party. I picked up two new clients. Jeremy sent them my way when they asked him who handled the marketing campaign.

I'm still doing work for Whispers of Grace and Rizon when they need it.

"Linny, are you saying what I think you're saying?" Athena jumps to her feet. "Oh my god."

"What?" Breccan looks at her. "I don't get it."

His entire world is football at the moment. He's got a difficult choice to make and regardless of what it is, he'll be moving when it's time for him to start college.

He's been offered full scholarships at several of the best schools in the country.

Jeremy clears his throat. I look over at him.

Since he told his siblings about our engagement three months ago, we decided that I'd be the one to tell them about this.

About our baby.

"We're having a baby," I say as I stare at the man that I love.

Zach jumps to his feet. "A baby? Are you serious? We're having a baby?"

"No shit?" Tears well in Breccan's eyes. "We're really going to have a baby?"

I slide to my feet when Athena rushes toward me. I hug her tightly.

Zach is next, and then Breccan.

I savor each embrace before I feel Jeremy's arms circle me from behind.

"Is it a boy or a girl?" Zach asks. "Do you know?"

"It's a girl." Jeremy's voice cracks. "It's going to be a beautiful little girl."

"What will her name be?" Athena moves to stand next to us, her eyes dropping to the front of my gray sweatshirt. "That's why you've been wearing baggy clothes, isn't it?"

I nod. "We wanted to be sure everything was okay before we said a word."

That was important to us both after Harmony suffered a miscarriage six months ago. She had been overjoyed at the prospect of having another baby. I was with her at Crispy Biscuit when she started bleeding. I rushed with her in a taxi to the hospital, but there was nothing that could be done.

I held her as she cried in the ER until Reuben got there.

I haven't told her about my pregnancy yet. I haven't told my dad either.

I will when I see him next week before he leaves for Florida.

We've worked hard to build a new relationship that's based on respect and love.

It's a step-by-step process, but we're determined to make it work.

He wants me to forge a bond with Mitchell, but I'm not ready for that. I may never be.

"We're going to name her Cassidy," I say quietly. "In honor of Jeremy's mom."

A week after I met Jeremy's siblings, he told me about his mom.

She had passed away a month before his eighteenth birthday.

Layan Cassidy had been a remarkable woman who loved her son fiercely. She'd raised him with dignity and compassion after her husband cheated on her with the woman who would eventually become his second wife. It never made her bitter. She only drew strength from it, teaching her son about loyalty and love.

"That's beautiful." Athena reaches for Jeremy's hand. "I think it's the perfect choice, Jer."

"Me too." He kisses the top of her hand.

"Did you tell Blythe?" Breccan laughs. "She stopped by yesterday with that big basket of fruit and told us not to eat it. She said it was for Linny."

We all look toward the large wicker basket in the middle of the dining room table that's filled with apples, oranges, bananas, grapes and a pineapple.

"For fuck's sake." Jeremy fishes his phone out of the front pocket of his jeans. 'She must have been reading my emails again. Linny's been sending me nursery design ideas."

"I want in on that." Athena smiles. "We can fill it with fresh flowers every day."

"Wedding plans first." Jeremy laughs. "Nursery plans second."

"You're getting married before the baby comes?" Zach steps back. "You don't have a lot of time."

We don't, but we'll make it work.

Bethy is headed back to New York in a week and my mom told me she wouldn't miss my wedding for the world. I want both her and my dad to walk me down the aisle so I can wed the man I adore before our daughter arrives.

"Let's get out the calendar and find a day that works." Breccan skims his finger across his phone. "I'm obviously the best man."

"We're doing dual best men." Jeremy points at Breccan and Zach. "I want you both right there beside me. That works, right?"

Their smiles say it all.

I turn to Athena, swallowing back the rush of emotion I feel.

"I know you'll want your sister to be your maid-of-honor." She tucks a lock of my hair back behind my ear. "I can design the flowers, Linny. I promise I'll make you the most breathtaking bouquet."

"Make one for you too."

Her eyes scan my face. "Why?"

"I want you to be my maid-of-honor."

"You do?"

I reach for her hand before I turn to face Jeremy, Breccan and Zach. "You are my family. All of you. We're in this together, for better or for worse, right?"

"It's the five of us against the world." Zach raises his arm in the air.

Jeremy's hand falls to my belly. "Six. It's the six of us against the world."

I reach up to cup his cheek with my hand. "I love our life."

"I love you, angel."

"We all love each other." Zach laughs. "We'll handle the dishes tonight."

Jeremy and I watch as his siblings disappear into the kitchen.

"We're really lucky." I look up at him. "How did we get this lucky?"

"You put on a tutu and tiara and stole my heart away." His fingers brush my chin.

"I still have that tutu."

"Are you fucking kidding me?" He pulls me closer. "Tell me you're serious, angel."

"It wouldn't fit me now." I look down. "I'm a little thick around the middle."

"You're the most beautiful woman in the world." His hand moves to my neck. "Let's skip the movie and you can model the tutu and tiara for me."

"We could skip the fashion show and take a bath. It has to be a warm bath, not too hot."

Lowering his voice, he tugs me toward the staircase. "Or we could skip the bath and I'll take you straight to bed and fuck you."

"Deal." I pop up to my bare tiptoes and kiss his mouth. "Will you always want me this much, West?"

"No." He shakes his head. "I'll want you more tomorrow, and even more next year. By the time we're eighty, we'll never leave our bed."

I throw my head back in laughter. "I'll hold you to that."

"You better, angel. You're mine for life and nothing is going to change that."

ALSO BY DEBORAH BLADON
& SUGGESTED READING ORDER

HUSH

BARE

WISH

SIN

LACE

THIRST

COMPASS

VERSUS

RUTHLESS

BLOOM

RUSH

CATCH

FROSTBITE

XOXO

HE LOVES ME NOT

BITTERSWEET

THANK YOU

Thank you for purchasing and downloading my book. I can't even begin to put to words what it means to me. If you enjoyed it, please remember to write a review for it. Let me know your thoughts! I want to keep my readers happy.

For more information on new series and standalones, please visit my website, www.deborahbladon.com. There are book trailers and other goodies to check out.

If you want to chat with me personally, please LIKE my page on Facebook. I love connecting with all of my readers because without you, none of this would be possible. www.facebook.com/authordeborahbladon

Thank you, for everything.

ABOUT THE AUTHOR

Deborah Bladon has never read a romance hero she didn't like. Her love for romance novels began when she was old enough to board the bus, library card in hand to check out the newest Harlequin paperbacks. She's a Canadian by heart, and by passport, but you can often spot her in New York City sipping a latte and looking for inspiration for her next story. Manhattan is definitely her second home.

She cherishes her family and believes that each day is a gift for writing, for reading, and for loving.

Made in the USA
Las Vegas, NV
14 January 2024

84374570R00151